Pieces of You

GLAIZA DE LEON

Pieces of You

Paperback Edition ISBN: 978-1-7636239-0-3

eBook Edition ISBN: 978-1-7636239-1-0

Published by Glaiza De Leon

First Edition: August 2024

A catalogue record for this book is available from the National Library of Australia

Editors: Callie Rickard at CJ Editing and Chloe Higgins at Booklyst Editing Services

Book Cover Design: Ann Joven at Artsbyannz

Illustrations: Ann Joven at Artsbyannz

Design and Typeset: Glaiza De Leon

Printed in Australia.

For all the broken hearts, the healing hearts, and every heartbeat in between.

Prologue

2012

Everyone seems to be less anxious than I am about the first day of Year 7. Although there are a few familiar faces from primary school, they've somehow clicked with others and formed new friendship circles already—almost too eager to fit in with the high school scene. As they pass by me, I wait for an invitation to join them, but instead, my existence instantly fades into the background. *It's okay,* I think to myself, as my feet wander the grounds that will be my new second home for the next six years. With every step, my stomach churns, until finally, I find a quiet spot far from all the noise.

Sitting alone on the cold, damp ground beneath the shade of an overgrown tree, I watch from afar as the reality of high school hits me. I wonder how easy it is for so many to make new friends when I can barely make eye contact long enough to hold a conversation. Did everyone really think I was going to make a huge change and pick up all these new ways to talk to people during the six-week holidays? How do I even start to tell Aunt Marge that I'm still the same old twelve-year-old me from before, with no interest in politics or trying to understand any of that stuff? Trying to fill the shoes of a grown-up isn't as easy as it sounds, especially when I don't feel like one. Yet, it seems everyone else got the memo, with their deep coral lips, expertly winged eyeliner, and hair perfectly straightened as if they've just stepped out of a salon.

Thankfully, there's always a novel in my bag, saving me from situations like this. I glance at my watch, and there are thirty minutes until lunch is over. Enough time to start reading *We Were Liars*, a book my sister Ara has begged me for weeks to read. She says she desperately needs someone to exchange thoughts with and pour her emotions onto. She hasn't been able to pick up a new book to read because her heart is still aching from it.

We're alike in that way—reading brings us closer together even though we're complete opposites in everything else. Ara is only two years older than me, outspoken, and the life of any party. She fits in with every group at school as though she's a chameleon easily blending in no matter the scene. And expressing her thoughts vocally? She has zero trouble doing so with anyone, even her teachers. One time her Year 9 English class spent an entire period watching a movie unrelated to their learning. Ara being the vocal person that she is, made her opinion known by telling Mr Keith why that wasn't productive if he ever wanted them to have a meaningful connection with the subject. Ara is a straight-A student as well, in every class. Yes, *every* subject. Usually, there's this idea that someone good at Maths and Science can't excel in a creative subject like Art, or fall behind in Home Ec. But not Ara. She's known as the Frida Kahlo and Giada De Laurentiis of the entire student body.

Meanwhile, you could compare me to a turtle. I have an invisible shell I'm more than happy to hide in. To be in the shadows, away from any spotlight. It's where I feel most comfortable. I'm okay with having fewer friends than my fingers can count, or being alone if it means less awkward interactions. In fact, as I sit here like a lone wolf in unfamiliar territory, I come to the realisation that my hope of belonging to a pack is history considering my only friends from Year 6 have had a change of heart.

And academically, well, I'd be lucky to receive a mark better than a C. I don't know what it is about sitting exams, but my anxiety heightens and my thoughts mesh into one. By the time I can think with clarity, the clock has ticked and all pens are down.

You could say I remain in the shadows with that, too.

It looks like I'm not the only shadow though because a shadow hovering over me quickly gets my attention and swerves my thinking off-guard. I take my eyes off the words on the page, and towards the figure whose presence would very much like to be known.

The person's face sends a nostalgic feeling from the past but I'm too stunned to gather my thoughts and track down the familiarity. Although standing confidently, there's a calming aura about him. The way his mouth arches without any effort. It doesn't seem to matter to him that he's seen near me, as though he's blocked out the glares coming from afar.

"It's a good read," he says.

I'm lost for words. Instantly, my vocal cords have been muted. He stands there, waiting.

"Can I sit with you?" he asks, not giving me enough time to gather my thoughts and somehow link them with my voice. Instead, I return my best effort with a friendly nod.

He smirks, amused by my expression and sits directly besides me. To my surprise, he pulls out the same book from his backpack, quickly unfolds the dog-ear folded around one hundred pages in, and then flips the book back to the very first page.

I struggle to slip a sentence out, and he recognises this. Based on my look of confusion, I can tell he's read my mind.

"I take it you don't like talking much?" he says this with the assured expectation of no reply. But he continues talking anyway. "I was just thinking ... Isn't it awesome how we can both sit here in absolute silence, once I stop talking that is, without even looking at each other, both eyes glued onto our books, and have the exact words running through our minds from the text we're reading? Pretty neat, huh?"

Wow, that's something pretty deep to say to a stranger. But I agree, and give another nod in agreement.

"I'm Lucas, by the way." He adds, "And you are?"

There's a long pause before I build enough confidence to say the word I never expected to say to anyone today. "Wynter."

Someone asked for my name.

1

Mum

3 Years Later: 2015

M RS HOPE PLACES THE paper face down onto my desk, without giving me any indication as to how I should feel about it. It tortures my mind, slowly and then at full speed. I hunch closer towards the edge of the desk in a not-so subtle attempt to hide the paper I'm about to flip over. The truth is, I'm afraid that others sitting behind me might catch a glimpse of it. This isn't a new feeling, but it gets to me each and every time. My nerves scatter throughout, further taunting my headspace.

I flip the page.

My pulse stops momentarily as I'm faced with a bright red F on the top of my second Maths test of the year. Not a great start to Term Two. If only I had insight into the secret formula on *How to score better than an F in Maths*. I mean, how could I fail so miserably? I spent the whole week studying for it, with both Mum and Ara using the very few spare hours they have to also help me. Trying to wrap my brain around the basic concepts of the world of numbers is like running through a series of never-ending obstacles, each one knocking me down. Now I regret not spending that time sleeping instead, because I could sure use a few extra handfuls of hours of that. The puffy bags nested under my eyes says it all.

"Can I speak to you after class?" Mrs Hope says softly, almost in a whisper.

I nod without looking her in the eye. I know she's disappointed in me, possibly even embarrassed. It's a hard truth to swallow.

Lucas quickly places his pencil case over his sheet to cover his perfect A score. He leans over to give me reassuring comfort through unspoken words. His eyes illuminate kindness, making it pretty obvious he's trying to make me feel less deflated. I return a sealed smile, knowing he sees right through it. My forced effort of smiling, I'd score an F, too. I struggle to shake this unwanted feeling off.

The whole class is sharing their results, and it only takes me a minute to work out that I'm the only student who has failed. I'm probably the only one who studied the most, too. The irony, right?

When the class is dismissed, Mrs Hope motions her way towards me. She has that look on her face. A look I know all too well. The way her head lowers and her eyes crinkle, coupled with the sound of soft sighs through pursed lips. The lack of eye contact is the icing on the cake. This look is far worse than a burst of anger because it intensifies and confirms the feeling of failure.

"What happened, Wynter?"

"I'm sorry."

There's silence—we're both lost for words. Our body heat radiates the space between us. Although my skin is quite tan, I'm pretty sure my burning cheeks turn as red as the F on my paper.

"I'm not angry, Wynter. I'm not even disappointed. I just want to know if anything is troubling you. You know you can tell me anything."

"Other than being ridiculously bad at Maths?" I say this too quickly, nearly as quickly as it takes for me to realise it's not the right time to be sarcastic.

"You're not bad at Maths, Wynter, it just takes practice. Believe it or not, but I was always only just passing Maths in Year 10, and got my fair share of F's too."

"What changed it? I mean ... you're clearly no stranger to Maths now."

"Well, I realised I was too focused on trying to remember everything to get a perfect test score. I just slowed down and focused on one thing at a time. To understand the thought process behind what I was doing. Even if it meant half of my test was perfect, and the other half seemed like it was completed by someone else. It's not a race."

"Thanks, Mum."

We hug it out, and my pulse returns to a normal rate.

Outside of school, everyone calls me Mini Faye because I look just like my mum. We could pass as twins with a 30-year age gap. But it's also clear that whilst we look identical on the outside, I most certainly did not inherit her brain. Mum is one of those teachers who get an end-of-year gift from every student. Her empathetic nature and calm presence makes her approachable, especially for a Maths teacher.

I remember one time she received a thank you card and a box of Ferrero Rocher from Olivia, the one person who manages to slip into detention by every other teacher because she's not exactly the best at sitting still and paying attention. Mum, on the other hand, really took the time to attend to Olivia's struggles and allowed her to go for a quick walk around the block if she felt the need to not stay still. Whenever she returned to the classroom, she was better focused and a lot more relaxed.

Another time, instead of Olivia going on her own, Mum got the entire class to join. It turned into a lesson about calculating time and distance. It was pretty fun. I could tell Olivia appreciated the gesture by the permanent grin she had stretched across her face for the rest of that day.

Empathy and patience. They're qualities I admire from my mum. She makes it look so easy, but if that were the case, then there would be more people around the world showing them. In high school alone, I can tell you now, they're hidden gems.

My mum, Mrs Hope, reminds me every day to 'count your blessings' and 'always choose kindness' which I try to keep at the forefront of my mind. Today, my blessing is that although I failed my test, Mum was there with open arms to reassure me that failing a test doesn't mean I'm a failure.

And so, here I am, off to Art class in a much more positive mental state than I was ten minutes ago. *Count your blessings, Wynter. Count your blessings.*

2

Wynter with a Y

WE TURN THE PAGE simultaneously, coincidentally. Normally, I'm a much faster reader, but I decide to read at a slower pace today. Not to match Lucas' speed, but to give my brain some time to slow down too, for no reason other than it feels right.

"Thoughts so far?" he asks.

"I'll let you know in another twenty or so pages."

"I'm telling you, I bet whatever the twist is, it'll blindside us both. I can sense it."

I respond with a playful eye roll. Lucas likes to think he senses everything and is the epitome of gut instincts.

"I'm predicting in another twenty pages, you'll be turning those pages back to your normal reading speed. It's going to get better," he says.

"For someone who loves to read, you sure do talk a lot to someone else who loves to read, trying to read."

He knows I mean this jokingly so he takes no offence. He chuckles and then dramatically points out that he's reading silently.

From the moment we began reading *We Were Liars* together, all those moons ago, we've continued on that same path. Reading together during lunchtime is what we spend ninety-percent of our time doing. Because we've been so consistent, we don't get teased for it anymore. Occasionally, we'll get an odd glare, but it doesn't phase us. To us, it seems productive to sit in quietness, reading instead. Any conversation we usually save while we wait for the bus after school. Realistically, we only need a few minutes to be up to date on each other's lives. There's only so much that can happen when your day-to-day life consists of waking up, going to school, and then going home. Whilst most teenagers our age do extracurricular activities outside of school like soccer or dance, Lucas and I spend every day after 3pm homebound.

Lucas is a self-taught pianist and plays like a professional. He'll be touring as a solo performer one day, he's that good. He's recorded a few compositions before, which he happily shares with me, though only after I've begged him just short of a million times. You could say I'm his number one fan.

On the other hand, I'm too embarrassed to share any of my pieces because they feel too personal, even if they're not. I once wrote a song about feeling angry when Mum opened the curtains on a bright summer's morning while I was still sleeping, letting too much sunlight blind me. I should probably mention that I'm an amateur musician in comparison, but it keeps me sane and it's the one instrument I'm coordinated enough to play.

As Lucas and I continue reading, the unpredictable autumn weather suddenly leaves water marks on our pages. We quickly get up to escape the rain. Lucas' curly hair starts to frizz instantly, but he couldn't care less. It's one thing I like about him. He's not vain at all, even though he's confident. If he were the type to stop and stare at his reflection whenever the opportunity presented itself, I would eye roll so much it would give me a headache. Thankfully that's far from the case.

He still cares about his appearance but chooses comfort over bizarre trends. His mum, Cora, does his wardrobe shopping, and he's never complained once about it. Even though the majority of his clothes are hand-me-downs from his older brother, Guy, he doesn't cause a fuss over it. Lucas is a replica of Guy, just a head shorter. It's uncanny when they're side by side. They've inherited their hair through their South African father, Junior, and their olive complexion from Cora, who is part Italian and part Indonesian—a rather interesting but beautiful mix.

I should probably properly introduce myself, too. Most people think I was born in winter as soon as they discover my name, but I'm an autumn baby. Autumn would have been a nice name too, though. It reminds me of the crinkle-cut leaves in beautiful hues of oranges and reds and browns.

My Dad, Ye-jun, is half Korean. His mum married an Aussie after they fell in love one summer. My mum, Faye, is Filipino but grew up in Sydney when her parents migrated all those years ago. Although I'm a mix of both cultures, I often feel lost between both worlds. The basic sayings are as far as my vocabulary allows, which in reality doesn't get me very far at all. I get it though. Mum was afraid I'd grow up living in Sydney not knowing how to speak English if she taught me a different language, and besides Dad, there's no-one on his side of the family who can teach me how to speak Korean.

My parents were married for four years before Mum finally fell pregnant with Ara. After my sister was born, it was one pregnancy loss after another. Mum says when she passed the first trimester with me, she felt both relief and excitement as they had always wanted a sibling for Ara, but there was a constant fear looming until the day she was able to hold me in her arms.

What Mum didn't realise, though, was on that very same day she would lose the first love of her life.

It was the day Mum's heart rejoiced and grieved all at once.

Mum said that she and Dad were struggling to agree on a name for me. That they'd always loved the names of the seasons, but I didn't look like an Autumn, which stumped them. Winter was their next preference, and although that's what the midwives wrote on my baby card placed above my hospital bed, Mum quickly asked them to change it.

"Wynter with a Y," she told them.

It wasn't until I had learned to read and write, did it occur to me that my common name wasn't spelt so commonly.

"Why is my name spelt with a Y, Mum?"

Mum recounted the story about the day Dad died followed by, "And because you didn't look like an Autumn, we chose Winter. I asked the nurse to change the I to a Y the moment I found out about your dad's tragic accident. That way, he would forever be a part of our lives, even if it was just in the spelling of your name."

The Y resembles Dad's name, Ye-jun. I much prefer it that way.

3

Moonlight Sonata

P**EPPER MAKES IT A** mission to greet me by the screen door. He's a funny old dog, it's never a dull moment when he enters the room. He's an eight-year-old miniature Dachshund with a signature waddle. Whilst Pepper is small and adorable on the outside, he most definitely puts the word protective on a whole new level. It's the only reason Mum feels comfortable with me taking Pepper on walks alone. If anyone were to attempt to harm us, he'd put them back into place. His fierce snarl and piercing eyes will have them running the opposite direction and Pepper wouldn't be afraid to hunt them down. It's no surprise since Dachshunds were originally bred for hunting.

"Hello, sweet boy." He reaches me and immediately rolls over for the, already expected, belly rub.

Without fail, he comes to a sudden halt by the staircase. Looking up at the steps, he lowers his head, dreading what's to come next. If Pepper had the choice, he would happily be carried up each time to avoid the unwanted expedition to climb Mt Everest. But today, his determination to shadow my every move makes this obstacle a mere challenge. Lifting his small legs, he waddles along upstairs by my feet, past Mum's precious Thai Constellation, her most prized indoor plant. It's a Monstera with white markings on it. Whilst I appreciate its beauty, I'm not sure I'd pay the price tag of three hundred dollars for a plant that will probably wither over time. But this sight of greenery, along with Mum's ever-growing collection, is worth every dollar because no matter how bad of a day she's had, all she needs is a few minutes wandering around the house, watering her plant babies, to ignite joy and a peaceful mind.

Pepper seems to agree. He has a routine of pausing briefly just as he passes it, as though he's taking a moment to soak its presence in too. That, or he just wants to sneak a nibble.

I flop onto my bed. It's been a long day. Pepper lays beside me, snuggling into a comfortable position. He nods towards the tissue box, which makes me smile.

"No, not today, Pepper. No tears. Just feeling overwhelmed. I don't know ... I know it was only a Maths test, but I just hate feeling like I'll never be good enough."

Before I slip another word out, I'm interrupted by the perfect performance of *Moonlight Sonata* from downstairs. Every key is played so effortlessly, you'd think Beethoven himself was the culprit. Ara plays, but she isn't a huge fan of classical music, so I know without a shadow of a doubt who this solo performer is.

I spiral down the staircase and lean against the wall to admire his talent. He looks up and notices me, but stays in character, like a true musician. When the song ends, Mum, who was already in the room, and I, both clap.

"That was incredible," we cheer.

"I've been practising all week. Mr Lennard says I need to work on conveying my emotions while I play," Lucas replies humbly.

"You definitely stayed in character," I say because he didn't flinch once.

Mum chimes in, "Do you know what the song is about or why Beethoven composed it?"

The long pause suggests Lucas hadn't thought about researching the song's history.

"Trust me, all you need to do is look into it and it'll be a challenge not to feel or show any emotion while you play. Mr Lennard will be fighting back tears. He's a big softie, despite his tough exterior."

Lucas smirks, knowing his Dad is the same. In Year 7, several students were so afraid of Junior they avoided befriending Lucas. Junior is close to two metres tall, with muscles protruding from every limb. Picture that along with an angry resting face and the deepest voice, it would probably make you look the other way, too.

Admittedly, he scared me the first time I met him. But Mum taught me better than to judge others based on appearances alone. Whilst I'm always cautious, I try not to jump to conclusions. Turns out, Junior is the most gentle soul on this planet. Like a big friendly giant.

"Thanks, Mrs Hope. I'll keep that in mind," Lucas replies.

Feeling accomplished, Mum beams from ear-to-ear before leaving the room.

"How 'bout you, Wynter? How's your composition coming along?" Lucas asks, shifting the spotlight to me.

"It's taking a lot longer than I thought it would. I need to be in the mood to write. At the moment every melody is sounding the same."

"What are you trying to write about?"

"That's the thing, I don't know. I've been trying to get a rhythm happening, any kind of tune. But without a topic, it all sounds off."

"Maybe just keep trying to play around with a few different tunes, then? Get your creative juices flowing."

"There's seriously nothing flowing. Which makes the whole thing feel more overwhelming. How can I not compose just *one* piece? Maybe I should just stick with a composition that's already been done. I'll have enough time to learn it."

"Don't even think about it. You're way too good of a writer to just perform something else. Don't let this eat you up. It's just *one* assignment which doesn't define your entire music career."

"Ha. Because I can totally step into the spotlight and become a renowned artist. You're forgetting who the true musician is here, Lucas."

"I wish I could help, but as cheesy as it sounds, the inspiration has to come from within. Then you'll write a winning piece for sure."

"And your inspiration led you to play *Moonlight Sonata* for your performance?"

"I'm hopeless with originals, remember? You know that. You've listened to every single one of them. I'm no songwriter. I'll stick with *Moonlight Sonata*."

"If you say so ... You don't give your talent enough credit. And I'm not just saying that because we're best friends."

"Talent is a funny word. Anyone can play the piano with enough practice ... Is it really a talent? Anyway, how did this turn into a conversation about me? There's one way I can think of that might be able to help you find inspiration ..."

"Which is ...?"

"Let's go for a walk."

"As long as you're back by dinner!" Mum yells from the kitchen.

"I guess that's a yes, then?" I say as I turn to Lucas to confirm.

It doesn't take Pepper long to figure out what's happening, so of course he's instantly by my feet wagging his tail in excitement as we walk along the hallway towards the front door. He loves walks, just like the next dog, but he also loves taking a hundred breaks within a short distance. I always have to make a mental note to time our walks according to Pepper's speed, because a thirty-minute walk often turns into an hour.

As the door swings open, I inhale the crisp, fresh air as we exit the front door. The gentle breeze is cold as it brushes against my arms, but the sun feels warm on my face. I'm briefly transported into a moment of calmness. But the moment ends all too soon when the sound of a siren whirs past from what seems to be a few streets away. It flicks an unwanted switch on, exposing the hidden pain I've been pushing aside. It leaves my heart looming in the dark. No matter how beautiful the world around me blossoms, it always feels incomplete.

I miss you, Dad.

I wish you didn't have to leave us so soon if only to be able to hear what your voice sounds like as I imagine you saying 'I love you' and calling me your little princess. I wish time wasn't so cruel as to steal you away so quickly. I wish the timeline of events shifted even just by a day, so the hour you left so suddenly wouldn't have been history.

As my mind wanders, I can see Lucas mouthing words without sound. I close my eyes to refocus, and as sunlight hits them again, I'm back to reality where Lucas' words are no longer muted. He's still talking, as though he couldn't sense my unintentional lack of listening, even if it was only for a minute.

"... I'm sure you'll get along just fine."

Instead of asking him to repeat everything he just said, I look at the path ahead and smile. Who will I get along with just fine?

A mother walking, holding onto a pram with what looks like a baby no older than three months, takes a quick break, scrambling for her bottled water. She looks exhausted, but that's probably from having a newborn as opposed to the walk. If anything, a walk is probably what she needs.

Mum has reminded me several times how tiring the newborn days are, and the countless sleepless nights she had, especially since babies can't differentiate night from day until they're a bit older. That meant rocking or breastfeeding me to sleep close to hourly until my feeds were stretched a bit farther apart. It didn't help that I soiled my nappy often overnight too, so I can only imagine how many nappies I went through.

On top of that, Mum had Ara, a toddler to also attend to. She made sure she tried her best to give us the same amount of attention because even a young child can feel isolated. Ara was hands-on when it came to me. Mum would ask her to get a new nappy, help pick my clothes, play peek-a-boo, and give me big sister hugs and kisses.

Mum says that although those nights felt endless at the time, she misses the chaoticness of it all. She's a self-trained super-mum when it comes to viewing the positives, even when her mind and body lacked enough strength from being sleep deprived. Every day she'd wake up yawning, whilst counting her blessings from the day before. She writes it all down in her journal and reflects on those moments when she needs a little boost for the day. So from a young age, she would recite affirmations and words of gratitude with Ara and I as we'd look at ourselves in front of the mirror. These days, it's so embedded in our daily routine, that it's the norm.

I am capable of loving and being loved. Today I am grateful for music. The healing properties melodies have.

For as long as I've known Lucas, he's been great with kids, and although he has an older brother, he's had a longing for a big family. Big enough to have the number of siblings required for a soccer team. Maybe he's subconsciously needed to fill that void by playing a big brother role to others. Without even thinking first, his instinct is to approach the mum with the warmest smile.

"What a sweet baby you have," Lucas says to the now-rehydrated mother. It's amazing how quickly a drink of water can bounce some-one right back up.

"Aw, thank you. James is our little pumpkin, although not too sweet when he keeps us up at night." She laughs whilst looking at James with a loving gaze.

"Hello, little one." Lucas waves his hand gently. "Aren't you a ray of sunshine?"

I know how much Lucas wants to hold James, snuggly in his arms. To whisper reminders of reassurance and hum a lullaby.

James has the chubbiest cheeks, it's hard not to be drawn to his adorable features. He looks so peaceful, as though nothing else matters as long as he has his mum within his view.

"It was nice to see you and James, it's added colour to our day," Lucas comments as we wave goodbye and let the mother continue on her way.

Added colour to our day. Maybe he somehow has insight into the inner workings of my mind. But he's right, baby James has made this monochrome world feel a lot less like that. Perhaps all I need is a daily fix of baby cuteness overload. I wonder whether I would have added colour to Dad's world.

"You didn't plan this whole scenario, did you? We just so happen to come across the most squishy baby on our walk for inspiration, in a neighbourhood that barely has any kids?"

Lucas holds both hands up to prove himself not guilty.

"Just a coincidence," he says. "A pretty cool one at that."

Pepper barks as the mum leaves. She's pushing the pram with a little more ease now that she's reached the downhill part of the street.

"Has anyone ever told you, you'd make the perfect dad one day?"

Lucas blushes but returns a hopeful smile. "I mean, it would be awesome having mini me's with their frizzy hair defying gravity as they ran."

"That would be adorable."

"One day ... Hopefully." Lucas shakes his head and quickly switches his frame of mind. "Now let's not get sidetracked. Have you ever thought about why you want to compose a piece without any lyrics?" Lucas asks, taking me back to the whole purpose of this walk—finding inspiration.

"Mmhh, I haven't really *lived life* to write about much. I don't know, there's something comforting about listening to an instrumental piece. The good ones anyway. The ones that pierce through your heart, get you real good."

"A little like *Moonlight Sonata*?" He raises an eyebrow.

"I guess you could say that. But I just can't seem to have the same sort of emotional outcome."

"Well, it wouldn't hurt to have an audience of one, right? Let me critique what you've got so far. I promise I won't be biased. And just letting you know, you've *lived life* more than you give yourself credit for. Sometimes, you just have to go back to square one to find the answer."

"Back to square one ..." I repeat almost in a whisper. "Lucas, you're a genius!" I pull Pepper by the lead back towards home as quickly as I can before the inspiration drifts away.

My pace picks up whilst Lucas trails behind. His appearance would make you think he'd be into every sport under the sun, but he's an absolute history geek, both modern and ancient, and he wouldn't be able to kick a ball for hours, even if his health depended on it. He has much longer limbs than me, but he walks at half the speed, so right now he's struggling to keep up. Without his trusted bicycle he's no faster than a tortoise.

I turn my head for a few seconds, feeling bad that this walk has turned into torture for him. We're only a street away from his house, so I motion for him to head home.

"I'll just see you tomorrow, thanks again!" I call out as loudly as I can, without losing focus.

Lucas scratches his head, slightly confused, and stops briefly to catch his breath.

"Okay!" He yells from afar, "I'll be expecting an update."

I allow my arched lips to flicker across my face to make itself known so that he knows he can count on me. I continue down the narrow footpath with my heart thumping as steadfastly as the thoughts brainstorming in my head. In just a few minutes, I'll be composing my best piece yet. I just know it.

4

Red

MY PEN GLIDES EFFORTLESSLY, filling the empty page. Composing a pure instrumental piece is out the window. Word after word, note after note, I keep writing. My hand muscles tense after several minutes, revealing its weakness, but I shake it off to loosen the cramped feeling and keep writing. Every creative bone in my body is on a high. It's the first time my thoughts are racing faster than my hand can keep up with. I hum a tune as I reflect on each written line. It's perfect. Until I write the word 'you'.

You. This shifts my focus towards the ceiling fan, spinning and spinning, mimicking the quickness of the loops circulating my thoughts. I can't help but wonder who that *someone* is that Lucas was referring to. Apparently, we'll get along just fine.

This person must be significant in Lucas' life because he doesn't normally leave suspense when it comes to introductions. He'll tell me in advance if he has a distant relative or friend staying at theirs so that it wouldn't surprise me when we'd meet. If Lucas did name this certain someone, I have to blame my wandering mind for missing it.

The fan continues to rotate in a rhythmic motion, tapping into my anxious mind. Sleeping it off won't work, my body just isn't designed to sleep things off, so I sit by the keyboard to continue working on my musical piece instead.

I strategically place my mobile phone near the keyboard, steadying it before pressing the record button. My fingers play the keys gently, stringing together the first part of the melody. I press the stop button and then replay the melody to review the composition to hear how it sounds as a recording. It's the closest to knowing how the introduction will sound to others, before it gets to the first verse with lyrics. Singing. It always ruins my recordings. My voice isn't noteworthy when you hear it in person, let alone recorded, where it makes me sound tone-deaf.

I record several times before I'm happy with the way the introduction sounds. Listening to it makes my heart ache a little, and I notice that I'm holding my breath longer than my lungs find bearable. My chest feels tight, but that's when I know for sure that this is the melody I've been trying to convey for many years now. I just need to convince myself that I can sing the verses.

A monthly calendar that hovers above my study desk reminds me that I have exactly two months left to complete this musical piece. Exactly two months to go until I have to perform this sentimental melody in front of the whole class. That thought alone sends a flutter of butterflies deep in my stomach. There must be thousands of them.

I am braver than I think, stronger than I feel. I have the courage to face my fears.

I recite this several times as my reflection in the phone's blank screen looks me right in the eyes.

***

Lucas and I arrive at the school gates just as the bell rings, and we turn in opposite directions to get to our classes. I head down the corridor to the Drama room. Mrs Yieldeman looks utterly impressed by her vibrant, colourful display of famous quotes on the board—an *inspirational vision board* as she calls it. She ducks into the storage room for 'one last thing' to present to us, hoping to skyrocket our motivation, because let's face it, nothing is exciting about acting a made-up role unless you were born a star.

Reality is hard enough to navigate.

"Well if it isn't Wynter, or should we call you, *Red*?"

It's Alison-Mae, A.K.A Ali, with her two inseparable side-kicks, Lea and Ivy. The whole class turns their attention to me, eager for a response. I look across at Penny who is telepathically begging me not to stay silent. She loves real-life drama, which explains why she excels in this class miles ahead of everyone else. Joeli catches my eye and laughs to himself knowing I have no chance against the three of them.

I avoid any eye contact with Ali as I struggle to think of a reply. I guess Joeli deserves credit for predicting my inability to stand up for myself. The pressure of finding the right words to say in public inevitably gets the best of me.

"Looks like Red's a bit of a mute today." Ali's voice continues to project loud enough for the entire class to hear, and they laugh in unison.

"Nothing new," Ivy adds on. She scrutinises me as though I'm a creature from another galaxy that has just descended on her planet.

"Nice cardi, Red. Did you steal it from your grandma's closet?" Of course, it's not a trio of insults unless Lea chimes in. Why is there always a trio of bullies, anyway? Would they still be who they appear to be if they didn't have each other's backs?

I want to say something, but instead, I feel overwhelmed with embarrassment. Why is the spotlight on high-beam over someone who chooses books over looks? On someone who prefers minding their own business instead of being in the mix of teenage drama? For a slight second, I see myself as the loser they believe I am. Words have a greater effect on me than I wished. It's as though my brain has decided to store every hurtful word in my memory bank and forget the good ones, like the occasional compliments from strangers. There are enough words in that memory bank to search synonyms for *weird*, that's for sure.

I am braver than I think, stronger than I feel. I have the courage to face my fears.

Articulating a sentence is a challenge when my mind has its own agenda. It's decided that now would be the perfect time to disconnect. Ali's about to hit me with more words when I am saved by Mrs Yieldeman who scrambles her way out of the storage room, holding a pile of bright purple paper in one hand and red in the other.

"Good morning my lovely students!"

Did I mention how perky Mrs Yieldeman always is? Her quirky nature makes her annoyingly likeable. She makes everyone feel important, even those who are drowned out time and time again by the outspoken ones. Her hair colour reflects the bright, positive person that she is. If it's not dyed purple, then it'll be a fluorescent pink, or a blue as deep as the ocean. One time, it was all the colours of the rainbow. But that's Mrs Yieldeman for you, as vivid and fun as every colour under the sun. Luckily our principal promotes individuality, so the colour of someone's hair isn't an issue.

Although I'm not a fan of Drama class, I have to admit, Mrs Yieldeman is at least a teacher who gives me comfort and never makes me feel like I don't belong, even if my acting skills can put an entire audience to sleep. It's one reason I selected the subject. That, and Mum thought it would help me with public speaking and getting to know others in a different light.

"I thought it would be a brilliant idea to write a letter to your future selves, stating all your hopes and goals for the year, what your current emotions are, any significant events happening, and whatever else you please. You can seal your completed letters in an envelope and I'll return the letters to you at the end of the school year so you can see how much has changed and how much you've grown and achieved. This will be so much fun!"

Her enthusiasm baffles everyone, except for me. I admire how she continues to find joy and a thrill for life in everything she asks us to do. I imagine it wouldn't be easy being in her shoes, considering I'm one of maybe three students who *want* to pass her class, even if acting is the last career I'd consider. Everyone else calls it a breeze because apparently, the art of acting is a lot easier than Chemistry or History or Maths, or even Geography. But let me tell you, stage fright and forgetting your lines at the final second is a real thing. Being under the spotlight isn't in my nature—it has the power to make me feel more awkward than I already am.

Ali raises her hand, and Mrs Yieldeman happily gives her permission to talk.

"Wynter's too shy but she wants to ask for the *red* paper."

She looks me straight in the eye with a raised eyebrow and an evil grin slowly spreads across her face. As if she's the conductor of an orchestra, she leads the class into hysterics. My surroundings start to blur and the room swallows me alive like I'm being sucked into a giant vortex. My ears fill with a rushing sound, muffling everything. Yet I can't ignore the heightened sounds of laughter, ringing louder by the second. I shut my eyes tightly, hoping to disappear, but there's no escaping Ali. I'm her target, and she's just scored a bullseye.

I often wonder what it would be like if the tables were turned. If suddenly Ali and her followers were the uncool ones. But Mrs Yiledeman is too wound up in her happy state to notice that Ali wasn't being thoughtful at all. She was making fun of me, especially with the emphasis on the word *red*.

This isn't the first time Ali has singled me out. Most students don't even know the 'red' history, so they're just laughing in agreement with her so they aren't the next target.

"Well of course you can, Wynter!" She glides towards me and places the sheet of paper on my desk.

Laughter ripples through the room with more force, and Mrs Yieldeman commands everyone to stop immediately, looking confused as to what sparked humour to begin with.

There's a knock on the door as everyone starts jotting down their letters. A girl dressed neatly in our school uniform wearing glasses to match her ginger locks and freckles stands tall.

"Oh hello there, Miss ... Stacey." Mrs Yieldeman is ecstatic, she's beyond words now. Her swift motion towards Stacey redirects everyone's attention to the new student.

Stacey's pale cheeks turn a rosy shade and her posture looks as though she's slightly uncomfortable about the whole ordeal.

"Please, darlin', take a seat." Mrs Yieldeman points towards a few empty spots near the front of the classroom.

With a nod, Stacey does as instructed, trying not to draw even more attention to her. Unlucky for her that the only spare seats are smack bang in the middle of the front two rows.

Ali takes it as her cue to be the first person to introduce herself to Stacey. She always gets in quickly whenever there's a new student. It's her way of sussing out whether they'll be part of her clique or not. I mean, it's such a small close-knit group, that nine times out of ten, newcomers don't even get the chance to get to know them.

Stacey's outward appearance reminds me of a mannequin posing at the front of a clothing store, so perfect that it could pull off any outfit, no matter the season or style. It's probably the exact reason why Ali approached her without any hesitation. For her, beauty is only what the eyes can see. Stacey's instantly a frontrunner because of her looks alone. It's a sad truth, and I'm hoping Stacey can prove Ali wrong.

"I *love* your glasses," Ali states with exaggeration. Knowing her since primary school, I know all too well that this means she hates them. I don't understand how she can lie so effortlessly, masking her true thoughts, whilst looking at you point blank in the eyes.

"Thank you," Stacey replies, straightening them out a little. "My mum got them for me as a little gift for our big move. To make it feel less daunting, I guess."

"Aw, that's super sweet. Come sit with us at lunch, okay?"

And just like that Ali turns back to her little clique and starts giggling as though they're the most fun people to be around. I wish I had the courage to step in and invite Stacey to sit with me and Lucas for lunch. It's not something I'd normally do because change can be scary. But there's an unsettling feeling running through my veins as though I'm obligated to save Stacey from joining the wrong crowd after witnessing one of Ali's unauthentic gestures.

Instead, I work on the task at hand, because as much as the rest of the class thinks it's lame, I find it therapeutic and perhaps eye-opening.

Dear future me …

5

TBR List

LUCAS' EYES ARE GLUED to his book, but it's obvious he's been reading the same lines over and over again. He isn't focused as he normally is. His mind is wandering far beyond the book's pages.

"Are you all right?" I ask.

There's a delay before he responds, "Yeah ... just struggling to get through this page."

"I'm struggling to get through this whole book to be fair."

"Just a few more days of it."

To date, we've read over forty books. We aim to read one book a month, even though we could probably double that if we wanted to. We made a commitment to finish whatever book we'd started, no matter how hard it is to continue reading. We both feel like it's the most respectful thing to do since the author spent many hours writing the story. I mean, it's a mammoth task for me to complete a 4,000-word short story in English class, let alone a novel with at least ten times the number of words.

"How about we read a few more pages and call it a day for now?"

"Sounds good," he replies and unfolds the dog-ear from the page that he's been stuck on.

"Oh, and before I forget," I say as I fumble through my bag, "I got something for you. Close your eyes and lay your hands open."

Lucas tilts his head like a lost puppy, unsure how to respond. The excitement inside me is masked by my absolute best at holding a poker face. Lucas does as instructed and shuts his eyes. As he does, his cheeks puff and a single dimple reveals a sense of joy. I place the gift on his steady hands.

"Okay, open your eyes."

Within a split second Lucas' eyes widen and the smile he's always worn widens too.

"No way! What?! Wynter ... This is the best! Thank you! How did you know?"

"How did I *not* know, you mean? You've only talked about this book since Year 8," I reply playfully. "I finally found a copy you can keep."

"It's a First Edition copy too!" Lucas is beyond ecstatic. "Thanks Wynter. This is officially the best book I own."

I've known for a while now that Lucas has been hunting down a copy of *The Robot Who Looked Like Me* but without any luck. The chances weren't promising since the publisher stopped printing newer editions. At every bookstore visit a few suburbs away, I'd ask Wendy if they had landed a pre-loved copy. The reply was always the same. It started to feel like asking was pointless, until yesterday morning. I answered the phone to hear the most memorable words from Wendy, "We've got a copy for you, dear." Mum only had to take one look at me to guess the good news. She didn't hesitate to drive me to the bookstore right away.

"Just ignore the cover, it's a bit creased."

Lucas inspects the book with a wave of exhilaration sweeping through him.

"It's perfect, Wynter. I like the creases. They add character."

"I'm glad you like it."

"I love it. And that you took note of me wanting a copy for so long now. Even if you didn't find one, just knowing you cared enough to try looking … It means a lot."

"Let's not get overly sentimental now," I joke. But the truth is, even if Lucas is the one beaming, it's my heart that's bursting with happiness. Elated is how I always want to see him.

Everything about this moment is priceless. His smile. His contentment. His grateful heart. I wish I could hit pause and replay this exact point in time again and again.

But I'm reminded that reality is different. Just as Lucas is about to flip through the pages, the sunlight is blocked by a tall figure. We look up, and she's there, arms folded, somewhat fragile and frail, but with a friendly stature.

"Hey … Stacey, right?" I say. I'm not normally the first to start a conversation, but Stacey doesn't appear intimidating, or judgmental for that matter. I figured saying a few words would make the fact that she remained standing there a little less awkward.

"Stacey?" Lucas calls out, slightly puzzled as he finally looks up from his book. He says her name as if this isn't their first encounter.

"Thought I'd find you somewhere away from the crowd," Stacey remarks. Her voice sounds calm. "Actually," she continues, "I'm trying to hide from this girl I met in class earlier today. I can't remember her name, but she seemed adamant about sitting with her group. I just … Well, you know me, I hate being *seen* too much."

Lucas turns his face slightly so that our eyes are in direct view of each other, then gives me the *'Can she sit with us?'* look. He knows I can tell what he's trying to say, facial expression alone, so I roll my eyes and return an, *'Of course, she can! But you invite her'* look and we both snicker just thinking about our whole telepathic conversation. Maybe we're long-lost twins with the way our minds connect.

"You're free to sit with us." Lucas motions. "Just a disclaimer though," he adds, "we're pretty boring people, according to everyone who sees us reading every day."

"You guys read every day during your breaks? *You* read every day?" Stacey seems surprised by the revelation that Lucas reads every day, or maybe by the fact that he even reads. I'm not sure what angle her shocked question came from, but his comment evidently caught her off-guard.

"Is it that unbelievable, even though I literally have a book in my hands?"

Stacey laughs it off and sits besides me. This is all new for me, because right now, other than knowing she's a new student, I know nothing else about her. I don't want to overwhelm her by asking too many questions and to be honest, I'm too shy to ask, so I introduce myself instead because that seems like a much easier sentence to spit out.

"I'm Wynter by the way. Wynter with a Y."

"You were in Drama class, right? I remember that girl ... umm."

"Ali." I'm pretty sure that's who she's referring to.

"Ah yes, that's it. Ali. I remember Ali making a big deal about you and the word red. I felt pretty helpless since I was still standing outside the room at the time with the Year Advisor. But her voice travels through the building, that's for sure."

"You're not wrong about that," I reply, trying to avoid explaining anything else that she mentioned. Even Lucas doesn't know about Ali calling me *Red*. I don't want to make a big deal about it. But from the corner of my eye I see Lucas' expression shift. His eyebrows are suddenly raised with concern. Without a doubt he's about to ask, so I cut in with a question.

"Where's your accent from by the way?"

"Oh. My family is from California, but we're living here in Sydney now, where I was born. It's a culture shock though, and I'm still trying to understand Australian slang. I was so embarrassed at the airport when someone approached me asking where Maccas was. I thought they were looking for a person."

That made me chuckle. Of course, though, how does McDonald's translate to Maccas? I have to admit that I only recently found out Americans say Mickey D's, so she's not entirely alone.

Stacey places her backpack on her lap and unzips the front pocket. She pulls out a very bright crocheted purse in pink and purple, with an Aztec pattern.

"Thankfully I take this with me everywhere I go," Stacey says as she pulls out a novel from the purse.

"Oh, you're a bookworm too?" I'm suddenly sitting up a lot straighter, and slightly leaning in to see the title of her novel.

"All day every day if I could," she says loud and clear.

"I've read this one so many times. I have this weird thing of reading two different books at the same time. This one I have in my bag at all times no matter where I go, even to the shops, and my second book lives in my bedroom under my pillow. That one changes often because I usually read a new book each week."

"Is that one your favourite? *Bridge to Terabithia?*" I ask, recognising the title. I have to admit, I've watched the movie many times, but I've never read the book. Which is quite embarrassing considering I refer to myself as a bookworm. I make it a mission to read the book first before watching its movie adaptation. It only makes sense that way. But I honestly had no idea that *Bridge to Terabithia* was based on a novel until this very moment.

"One hundred percent. I've read it so many times, I don't need a bookmark for it anymore, that's how well I can memorise the page number I'm up to based on what part of the story I last read. Do you like it as well?"

Lucas smirks a little and decides to chime in, "Our little book club of two has never actually read it. But we've watched the movie hundreds of times."

Stacey is as still as a statue, jaws dropping to the ground. "What? Please tell me you're joking. I did not just join a book club that hasn't had the most spectacular book of all time, in my very honest but humble opinion, as part of their TBR list."

"He's not joking," I add. "You've caught us red-handed."

Lucas and I shrink into our imaginary shells as we notice Stacey's eyes widen in genuine shock. She's questioning the validity of this book club of ours. I'm expecting another string of words from her now not-so-shy-mouth, but instead, we all break into laughter until our stomachs hurt.

Our book club of two has now become a book club of three. And *Bridge to Terabithia* will be pushed to the top of our *To Be Read* list. Our very own TBR list.

6

The First Time

We're all huddled by the bus stop like a can of sardines. Attempting to squeeze my way through the crowd is impossible. I don't understand why everyone is so concerned about being the first on the bus. I get that there are the 'cool' spots further at the back, but is it worth suffocating in all this sweat and invading everyone's personal space bubble in return?

Lucas manages to find me practically trampled by the much bigger teens.

"I take it now's not a good time to talk?" he says.

"We can only try. Maybe just try and save me a seat instead? There's a higher probability of you getting on the bus before me."

"Look at you being a mathematician," he jokes. The realisation makes me want to give myself a pat on the back though. Where's Mum when I'm incorporating Maths into my life and actually using it correctly?

Lucas' comment makes me laugh and momentarily forget that I'm being swallowed alive by a swarm of teenage kids who think it's a battlefield to hop onto a bus. I don't even know how I became entangled within this. Lucas and I are usually several metres away from the crowd, so that we can, at least, hear our thoughts. That ten minutes of peace is a lot better than ten minutes of scrambling just to get a seat. That peace makes up for the entire bus ride home where Lucas and I are normally standing because we're always the last ones on, meaning zero empty seats left.

After several more minutes of being within the vicinity of every cologne and Impulse body spray, I finally find refuge with the arrival of the school bus. When its doors open, I picture David Attenborough observing from nearby, narrating the scene: *A colony of ants march their way into the vehicle, focusing on their mission to invade every crevice of its insides. Two ants trail behind, not displaying the same qualities of that as the others.*

Lucas looks at what unfolds before him and knows to pick his battles wisely. Today is not the day to fulfil my probability analysis. Today is not the day we secure any form of seating. Lucas turns towards me and face-palms himself knowing that the glimmer of hope to get a seat is out the window. It seems like such a dramatic thing, but because it's such a rarity for us to sit down on a bus, it feels like the most precious gift when we do. Today we are giftless.

We're standing in the aisle, between the seats, and I can feel Ali's presence looming over me from the very back seat. It's her spot, and everyone knows not to even consider sitting there unless you're granted permission, which is hard to come by. Even on days she's away, people are still too scared to sit there. So some days, a precious seat is left unused, even as many of us are standing. On one occasion a Year 7 kid sat there when Ali was absent and the news travelled to Ali by the time the kid got off the bus. Ali was so angry that her spot was invaded, she made it her goal to make it clear to that kid that *no one* sits on her throne. That poor kid endured a whole day of torture for doing something so minuscule—something that shouldn't have been an issue to begin with, and by far shouldn't have even reached Ali. Unworthy news travels fast.

For a reason unknown to mankind, I'm Ali's favourite person to pick on. Sometimes it's a small remark here and there as she walks past me, or in class, but on the bus, well, that's a whole different story. She makes it her sole purpose in life to make every bus ride a living nightmare for me. From 'accidentally' throwing her sandwich at me, smack bang on my hair, to gossiping untrue words about me so loudly that even the bus driver could hear, yet remain quiet like the rest of us in her firing line, and to getting her accomplices involved with tripping me over several times whilst trying to simply make my exit.

If that isn't enough, Lucas feels helpless. Unfortunately, although he isn't one of Ali's targets, she has enough of the male population on her side, under her wings, that it makes it tricky for Lucas to step in. He isn't a violent person, but he knows Ali's followers will easily resort to that if their status is trodden on by a mere defenceless Lucas. Without needing confirmation, we feel each other's pain. We both hope the bullying will come to an end before we graduate. The couple of times Lucas has tried defending us, Ali would reply by mimicking us, belittling us in front of whoever was around, even teachers.

Today, Ali has something else that I see from a distance, which makes me want to instantly leap towards her and snatch it out of her hands. It's too late. With eager eyes and lips curved with deceit, she holds the red paper above her head, waving it abruptly to bring it to everyone's attention, especially mine.

My eyes are already tearing up. I hate my inability to just walk up to her and demand it back. It feels like a moment of weakness, like I let her win.

"Dear future me, Wynter ..." Ali declares loudly as all eyes remain on her and my letter from Drama class, held tightly in her hands.

She continues without a grain of guilt, just pure joy and satisfaction. The way she reads each word aloud is with ridicule. Her intention is clear. Her motive is to embarrass me as she projects my innermost thoughts loud and clear so that even the poor, helpless bus driver, Arti, has to endure it. The one instance where Arti stood up to Ali, asking her to stop tormenting other kids on the bus, she retaliated by persuading her parents to report him to the school for harassment. Now hanging by a thin thread, even just one word to Ali could result in Arti's termination.

Ali clears her throat before continuing, "What's there to say ... I'm in Year 10. I feel like nothing much has changed about me since Year 7. I don't know why I'm not like everyone else who's trying to *find* themselves or *change* to fit in. No matter how many times I convince myself to 'be normal like them' I end up crawling back into my shell and failing any decent attempt at being someone other than what the world sees as my uninteresting self. I never realised how hard liking yourself would be until I started high school. But here I am, still the same old me, struggling to pass my grades in every class including this one. Why can't I just pass any class? Just *one*. To finally know how it would feel to see a proud smile on Mum's face as she hands out my test score with a PASS. I'll finally know how Ara feels every time it happens to her, which is *every* time.

"I still love reading and how Lucas and I have kept up with our lunchtime reading routine. It's still the highlight of our days. To others we're weird because of it, but to us it's weird that they care enough to give their two cents. We're currently reading a murder mystery which isn't usually a genre we'd pick. It popped up as a recommended book on Goodreads and well, we thought we'd see whether we could handle it. I have to admit, it'll probably be the first and last murder mystery I'll read. My heart and mind can't handle the suspense and intensity of it all. Sometimes I struggle to get through a page because the plot starts to slow down for far too many pages and at other points the gory scenes are too graphic. I'm yet to hear what Lucas thinks, other than he's struggling to get through it too.

"Besides that, I've been trying to make myself believe that I'm a good enough performer and I can kick my nerves out the door when it comes to presenting my musical piece in front of the whole Music class. If only I had as much faith in myself that Lucas has in me. I sometimes wonder what he really sees in me. And *how* he can be so certain that I'll do well. I'm so thankful for him ... With the limited time left to write a piece, I'm so glad Lucas helped me find inspiration. I don't have a love life, I don't go on crazy, daring adventures, and I don't have a lot of friends either, so yeah ... inspiration is hard to get by. When he said to think back to square one, it wired my brain to rewind time to the beginning, when Dad was in the picture.

"Mrs Yieldeman is confident that when I read my letter at the end of the year, it'll unlock happy memories. Every happy high school memory I've had to date is quite literally moments I've spent with Lucas. I know it might sound lame, but he's the reason getting out of bed each morning is a tad bit easier. He's the smile I look forward to as I walk into the school gates. He's the voice I can't wait to hear, even if it's just a recap of his book reviews. Because when Lucas is around, I know that I have someone on my side. He's my safety. A forever friend.

"I guess high school is far from rainbows and butterflies. It's more like a game of Snakes and Ladders. Just when you think you're doing great, a spanner is thrown in the works and you're sliding back down, the positive light of hope dimming as you do. If I could combine all my hopes for the rest of the school years, besides passing my classes, it would be to no longer hear the word *red* coming out of Ali's mouth. I'll never forget the day the name came to be. I just didn't think it would leave a permanent scar. Believe it or not but Ali and I were friends once upon a time in Year 5.

"One day, we were playing handball with Wren and Riley, and as I bent over to hit the ball, Riley started laughing and Wren's natural reaction was to join in until they were both in stitches. I had no idea what was wrong until they started steering away from me as though I was some sort of contagious disease. Surprise surprise, it was the very first visit of Aunt Flow. Because it was mufti day, you could see the red mark on my cream shorts as bright as day.

"I approached Ali for comfort, but my heart sank when she joined the others repeating the words, "Red, red, ew ... Red." Although there were only a handful of kids chanting along, the fact that my then-best friend didn't console me stung even more. The sharp, burning pain swelling around my chest still feels fresh each time I hear the word *red*. I've never felt that embarrassed in my whole life. The humiliation left me feeling extremely self-conscious. The day Mum always prepared me for, when I was supposed to step into 'womanhood' and feel great, was the day I felt small and defeated. After that incident, Ali joined a new circle of friends, and started teasing me up until this very day."

There's more to my letter, but Ali stops and says, "This is such a lie ... Any way to get attention. What a sob story."

She folds the letter back up, ushering one of her minions to return the letter to Mrs Yieldeman's class tomorrow before she notices it's missing. The rest can remain sealed and unannounced to suit her narrative. Lucas intercepts, grabbing the envelope, and looks at Ali straight in the eye. His gaze says enough without needing any accompanying words. For a brief moment, Ali freezes. To everyone's surprise, Ali is momentarily lost for words. That moment ends too soon as she presses the buzzer and says, "Move out of my way," with a deliberate nudge to my shoulder. She hops off at the next bus stop, even though we all know her stop isn't until another five stops.

"Come on, let's get out of here." Lucas comforts me, wrapping his arms around my shoulder as we walk to the front of the bus ready for the next stop. When Arti pulls over, he turns to me with sorry eyes.

"I'm sorry you had to go through that," he says. I return a gentle nod to reassure him that I appreciate his words.

"Don't worry about Ali, she's just trying to feed on your kindness," Lucas says, consoling me.

"Thanks," I murmur, trying with every might in my muscles to flex a smile.

"What are friends for, right?"

"At least you're not pulling off an Ali on me ... You didn't join in when everyone else laughed on the bus. Really, thank you."

Lucas shields me with his protective hold, wrapping me in his gentle arms. This is the first time in our entire friendship he responds with an embrace. He knew it was exactly what I needed then and there to not break down and cry, even if I didn't know it myself.

"Just remember, you'll be employing her one day."

The thought of that snaps me out of the humiliating ordeal. It even makes me smile.

7

Gone

ONE NEW NOTIFICATION. I'VE probably logged into Facebook three times since opening an account two weeks ago, mostly because Ara was so fixated on *everyone* needing a profile that she made one for me. Being so popular, she has over five hundred Facebook friends, but in reality, she probably only truly knows less than fifty of them. Meanwhile, I have twelve Facebook friends. Besides Ara and Lucas, the rest are distant family.

1 New Friendship Request from Stacey Jones. I click on the profile picture which confirms it's the same Stacey who joined our book club. We have one mutual friend, Lucas, which makes sense. Lucas is on Facebook a lot more than I am, mostly sharing random memes.

I click on *Accept* and within ten seconds, there's one new message sitting in my Messenger chat box.

Stacey: *Hey!! :)*
Wynter: *Oh, hello.*
Stacey: *I wasn't sure it was you since you don't have a profile pic. But Lucas confirmed. What are you up to? I didn't see you guys after school today.*

Wynter: *I'm not great with photos. Sorry, we were hidden amongst the bus crowd ... again.*

Stacey: *All good, maybe tomorrow we can meet up somewhere first? I caught the wrong bus home. Ended up walking for roughly an hour. So, Mum's been driving me to and from school since. She thinks I'll burst into anger if I keep getting on the wrong bus.*

Wynter: *I'm so sorry! It didn't even cross my mind of the possibility you'd be lost.*

Stacey: *You guys can make up for it tomorrow haha.*

Wynter: *Sounds good, see you then. I need to do some homework now.*

Stacey: *You're too studious ... See you tomorrow.*

Wynter: *A studious student who fails every class. The irony haha. Cya.*

I can't believe I completely forgot to check on Stacey to see if she'd be okay navigating the buses after school. There are around ten different school buses, so that's ten different routes. Catching the wrong bus could take you five suburbs away from where you live. Poor Stacey, she must have been panicking trying to find her way back home.

Placing myself in her shoes, I imagine how I'd react if I had to trek for an hour to find home. In a new country, a new city, and a whole new transport system. In all the American films I've watched, the bus driver stops in front of the person's house. If that's the case, what if Stacey thought the same thing happened in Sydney? That she was waiting for the bus to pass by her street and stop directly in front of her house. Thinking about it, I'm glad that's not the case here though. I'd hate for others to know where I live. It would give them the initiative to run by with a carton of eggs.

As my thoughts return to reality, I remember that Lucas wanted to talk to me, but being within a stampede wasn't the best place to converse and he hasn't brought it up since. Hopefully, he'll bring it up at school, although I'm tempted to message him instead. I tend to communicate better in writing because it feels less intimidating and you can hide behind your screen or paper. I let that thought pass over and decide Lucas should choose how he wants to convey whatever it is he has to say.

***

The school hallways are less busy; there's a slight reverberation amongst the whispers. There's an obvious drop in attendance during the colder months when colds and flus come to a peak. It doesn't help that our school uniform barely keeps us warm. Even with layers on, it still feels as though the wind is blowing straight through. Pretty sure my skin is covered in goosebumps, even beneath the thickest stockings I could find.

"Hey, Wynter!" Stacey calls from the other end of the hallway, rubbing her hands together to generate some heat.

I wave instead of yelling back, because attempting to use a louder voice from that much of a distance away gives me anxiety, especially since I'll most likely have to repeat myself thanks to my natural lack of volume.

We meet in the middle and Stacey leans in for a hug.

A hug.

Lucas only just hugged me for the first time two weeks ago and we've known each other for years. Stacey's hug causes an awkward jolt down my spine. It's probably all in my head, being the overthinker that I am. She's just naturally affectionate. I make an effort to appear less paralysed by the sudden and unexpected gesture.

"I made it to school on my own today," she announces proudly. "Without getting lost."

"That's so good. I'm so sorry again. I swear it wasn't intentional, it just slipped my mind completely. I shouldn't have assumed you'd know how to catch the buses here."

Stacey laughs. "Honestly, it's okay. I didn't tell you to make you feel bad, I thought it was a pretty funny story. I mean, it didn't cross my mind either that catching a bus here isn't the same as the U.S."

"Well, I'm glad you're looking at the bright side of things. It's refreshing."

"You either laugh or cry, right? Where's Lucas by the way? Or is he running late?"

"I was wondering the same thing. He usually arrives before me. He catches an earlier bus. Maybe he slept in. I'll message him."

My mobile phone is in my backpack because our school uniforms aren't designed with secure pockets to house them in. There's one pocket on my blouse, but it ends up putting too much weight and pulls the top down slightly, making it feel uneven and uncomfortable. So instead, I keep my mobile in a zipped pocket inside my bag, I guess it's safer there too.

Hey Lucas, are you coming to school today? I hope you're okay.

I keep my mobile out in case Lucas replies straight away, but the phone stays silent. As the school bell rings, Stacey and I part ways, heading off to our Homerooms. If Lucas shows up, I'll see him in English during first period.

There's a restless feeling deep within my stomach whenever Lucas is away. Not because I'll be by myself during recess and lunch, but there's a fear that lurks, the *what if he doesn't return?* He barely has days off school. What if running late by even just a couple of minutes leads to a horrible accident? Just like Dad. Mum says I need to worry less about these scenarios because it's not good for my health. But it's easier said than done. It's so hard to shut these thoughts out of my mind.

"Wynter, your mobile phone shouldn't be in sight," Mr Finn calls out.

"Sorry." I quickly check my phone for a message, but the screen is still blank. It's in my bag by the time Mr Finn looks back, giving me his nod of 'thanks'.

On the way to English class, I'm constantly looking over my shoulder in hopes Lucas' presence will give me the reassurance that my mind needs. I notice Sheree and Victoria and a few others from Lucas' homeroom walking together from the same direction. But there's no Lucas in sight.

As we line up waiting for Ms Walker to arrive, I muster up the courage to ask Victoria if she's seen Lucas. It's a struggle for me to walk up to her and find a way to interrupt the conversation she's having with Sheree.

I stand in front of them, awkwardly, with the same manner of a lost sheep. It's better than standing there without any form of expression. This is what I tell myself anyway to feel better.

They pause whatever it is they're talking about and both turn to face me. Unlike Ali, Sheree and Victoria are nice and have never been mean to me, even though they are popular in their own ways. They both excel in all subjects, academically, just like Ara and are friends with her because they've spent time together on the debate team and as SRCs.

Victoria starts talking with an empathetic tone, "Oh, hey, Wynter."

"Hey."

"Sorry to hear about Lucas. We only found out this morning."

My heart stops.

My mind explodes.

My body freezes.

Sheree speaks calmly, "I'm really sorry. Let us know if you need someone to sit with."

My mouth feels glued together because the pressure weighing on my heart stops me from physically being able to do anything. My thoughts go racing to the worst-case scenarios right away until it hurts my brain.

When Ms Walker stands at the front of the line, she looks straight at me with sorry eyes. Straightening her top, she approaches me and instructs the rest of the class to enter the room and do some quiet reading while they wait for her.

"Wynter, if you need some time away from class, we all understand. Principal Lee's aware and you have his permission."

Before I'm able to find my voice, I hear swift footsteps approaching me from behind. I can tell by the sound alone that they are running towards me.

As I turn, it's Mum who greets me with warm loving arms. Instantly, she embraces me, nesting my head on her shoulder.

The moment is puzzling.

Time stands still.

Everything around me blurs.

My head is spinning.

The impact of her hold makes me feel both at ease and terrified. Why has Mum left class to see me? She's always taken being a school teacher seriously and has never allowed a personal matter to get in the way during school hours. If something is troubling me, she knows to speak to me during our breaks, or as soon as we get home. The fact that she left class first thing in the morning to come and see me is concerning.

Mum's heartbeat thumps along with mine. I can feel the fast rhythm as she continues to embrace me. She's squeezing me so tight as though it's not her intention to ever let me go. As she does, we take a moment to analyse each other's expressions.

"Oh dear ..." Mum sighs. "You have no idea, do you?"

This revelation starts an onset of tears down her weary eyes. Often when someone starts to cry, it triggers the empathetic part of my brain and makes me cry too. But right now, my brain is still in a pile of confusion. Whilst seeing Mum in tears isn't a beautiful sight, I'm dreading to find out the reason behind it. I don't bat an eyelid. I try with all my willpower to not feel any emotion that would lead to the same result as Mum's unending drops of pain.

"Wynter ..." Mum's voice is fragile, the same way she sounds after a long jog, only this time in a much more frail and mellow tone.

"Mum, why is everyone saying sorry to me about Lucas? What happened? What am I missing? What does everyone know that I don't?"

At this point, no-one is silent reading. Even Ms Walker can't sit still. Every pair of sorry eyes are on me. The spotlight is blinding and I just want to scream at the top of my lungs for this nightmare to end.

I pinch myself even though I know I'll feel the pain. I pinch myself again, knowing that this is still the reality. I pinch myself a third time in hopes the first two tries were just a part of this make-believe day. I pinch myself again until Mum stops me from harming myself.

"Wynter, there's no easy way to say this. Lucas ... He ... He just wanted ... Ah ... Wynter, Lucas is gone."

"Gone? The cops are finding him though, right? We can help. Why are we at school? Mum, we need to—"

"Wynter, he's *gone*."

An amplified whooshing sound my ears can't escape echoes so loudly that it keeps me from standing still. My centre of gravity feels off-balance. When someone is gone, it doesn't mean they're gone for good. They can come back. They might be gone for just a few minutes, a few hours, or a few days ... But gone doesn't necessarily mean gone *forever*. Why would Mum say he's gone if he's not really? Why is everyone making a huge deal about Lucas being gone? He's not gone forever. Lucas is never gone forever. Lucas knows to always come back. He's the only friend who always ever comes back.

Lucas is not gone.

I walk into the classroom, pull out my novel like the rest of the class, and commence silent reading. I don't look up, not once, even though I can feel everyone's movements around me. No-one attempts to approach me—no-one knows how. They expected a different reaction. But no-one understands except for me, that *Lucas is not gone*.

8

Voicemail

EVERYONE MOVES ASIDE, MAKING a clear path for me. For the first time in four years of high school, I'm the first person to step foot on the bus. I don't take notice of this act of kindness, knowing they're only doing it because they believe my best friend is gone. As I enter the bus, and peer at the empty rows of seats, it doesn't feel right. I let everyone pass me and the seats quickly start to fill up, until there aren't any left.

Kasey and Evan and Jason and Becky and Willow and Sasha and a few other faces I can't quite fit a name to, offer me their seats. My wordless reply lets them know that I'm fine standing. Year after year I've been standing, with Lucas' hold always ready to keep me upright whenever my balance is shaken by the sharp turns. Only because Lucas is away today, it doesn't mean my routine all of a sudden changes. He's the one who wanted to save me a seat, not these other people who only know me by face and nothing else.

When the bus travels along the road closest to my street, I press the buzzer and walk towards the front of the bus. Arti slows down steadily and before I make my way off, he turns to face me with the same sorry eyes the rest of the school body is giving me and says, "Lucas was a good friend."

"He *is*," I say, and hop off. Normally I'd be inclined to shrug it off and let it be, but I couldn't just let it go, no matter how nice of a person Arti is. If there's anything English has taught me, it's that there's a clear difference between *was* and *is*. One is past tense. Lucas is and still is a good friend.

My body feels hot the entire walk home from the bus stop even though the air is crisp. With every step, a stabbing feeling lingers through my chest. The sky is just as sombre along with the thick clouds signalling a downpour.

Lucas can't be gone.

I look over my shoulder but Lucas isn't there, just autumn leaves swirling in circles, dancing along to the winds of change. The same way Lucas and I once did. Remembering this stings my heart and I start to lose feeling in my hands.

And then the rain falls. One drop at a time. Until it's so heavy that my tears get lost in them. I feel isolated, alone, confused. How do I function without the better half of me? How can I face the world without his footsteps walking alongside mine?

As thunder strikes, birds flee to nearby trees, but my pace remains slow and steady. My body is being dragged across the narrow footpath of this empty street, while my heart is being left behind. It no longer beats a hopeful melody. It just beats for the need to survive.

When I approach our front door, my body trembles. The water drips from my drenched skirt onto the porch, leaving a clear trail of my misery. I notice the screen door is already unlocked. Swinging it open, it's Ara who emerges from behind.

Her mouth is open, but silence fills the air. I wonder whether she's trying to form the right words to say, if there are even any. Instead, her glassy eyes meet mine with deep sorrow. Her mouth arches down, and her composure releases a long breath.

"You're home already?" I ask, breaking the quietness between us.

"I thought ... maybe you'd need a shoulder to lean on?"

"For?" I snap back, regretting the anger in my tone right away.

"Wynter ... I know it's not easy to accept. I can only imagine what you're going through. But I'm here for you."

"But you have debate practice. You need to be there, not here." My shoulders brush past Ara's in hopes the conversation ends and looking her in the eye can be avoided.

"You're more important than that, Wynter." Ara grabs me by the arm, stopping me in my tracks. My mission to avoid this confrontation felt so close, yet now I've landed so far.

"I'm okay, Ara. Thank you for thinking of me, but everything is okay."

"Wynter, you just lost your best friend. Everything is *not* okay. Maybe things will be okay a year from now, maybe five years from now, but right now, today is not okay."

Lost. Now Lucas is lost. He's gone, now he's lost. What's next? Why is everyone trying to be gentle and choose words like 'gone' and 'lost' as though they're going through a list of synonyms?

"He'll be back, Ara. Lucas always comes back. You know that," I say with a clenched jaw and a stare that makes Pepper run from beneath Ara's legs towards the opposite direction. Pepper's soft whimpers from the distance aches my heart, and leaves me confused and angry at the person I'm becoming.

"I know it's hard, Wynter, but you can't deny that he's not coming back. You're only hurting yourself even more."

"Then where is he? Is he *gone*? Is he *lost*? Why is everyone giving me this attention? Everyone who's anyone, some who only know me by face, nothing else. Why is everyone so concerned about Lucas being away for *one* day? No-one has ever cared about him other than me. No-one has ever cared if he was absent. No-one." Now my fists clench too, and my nails dig into my palms. It hurts. But numbness starts to take over.

"He was on his way to give you this." Ara's voice is gentle now. She pulls out a shiny CD marked with my name in Lucas' barely readable handwriting. "He shouldn't have been riding his bike so late in the evening, but his parents said it was important to him that it got to you. He was hit by a stolen Ute, and a P-plater was driving it after a night of drinking."

A P-plater? After a night of drinking? Lucas is not here because of a stupid drunk driver whose life is apparently more important than the one he just took. How is it fair that he gets to continue breathing in the air that Lucas' lungs can no longer inhale? It's not fair.

Ara hugs me as only a big sister knows how. This is when I break down and cry. I ugly-cry the same way I did in *Titanic* when Jack's icy cold hand slips away from Rose's grip and *My Heart Will Go On* starts playing, adding to the waterworks. I ugly-cry the same way I did in the movie adaptation of *Bridge to Terabithia* when Jesse finds out Leslie died trying to swing across the creek while he was busy spending the day with their teacher instead. I ugly-cry the same way I did in *My Girl* when Thomas J is stung to death by a swarm of bees trying to look for Vada's mood ring and Vada screams out at his funeral that he can't see without his glasses.

Lucas has slipped away from my grip.

I ugly-cry in Ara's arms until my body starts to shake and my chest sinks in, making each breath laboured. My cheeks burn, my stomach is turning, and my eyes lose focus. Everything around me is hazy, like one giant blur.

I escape from the comfort of Ara's warmth and run upstairs. My footsteps are heavy, just as heavy as an avalanche that traps my entire body. The door slams shut.

Standing still with my back against the door, I do what I should have done several hours ago. My scream is piercing and I imagine it causing the glass to shatter, but the only shattered object is me.

"Why?!" My cry for an answer is so loud and clear, but the answer remains a mystery. My back slides down the door, exposing my weak body. It feels numb to stay upright.

My tears turn into rage. It's not fair.

I can hear whispers from downstairs, voices trying to tread gently around me. Mum's home now—the distinct sound of her keys dropping onto the kitchen bench is a daily occurrence. She's usually home much later though. There's consistently an after-school meeting or extra tasks on her never-ending to-do list. But not today. The only thing on her to-do list is to come home to her daughter. But right now, my emotions feel too entangled to face anyone.

There's a soft knock on my door which I'm still leaning against. Sitting alone on the cold hardwood floor reminds me of the day Lucas and I met. Now there's a forever empty space besides me, and the sound of pages turning swiftly beneath his hold has become a distant memory. I'm angry at myself for not telling Lucas how important and what a star of a friend he was. That there was no other person in this universe like him. That there'd be no other being in this life that could ever take his place because Lucas came and marked a permanent special spot in my heart. He was and will forever be my best friend. Even if it means having to go years to make sure his face and the sound of his voice will never be erased. I promise myself that Lucas will not fade over time.

"Wynter, sweetie … can we talk?" There's a crackle in Mum's voice, trying her best to keep it together.

I don't want to be consoled. Sympathy isn't what I desire right now. As much as I love Mum beyond measure, I can't find the strength to talk, because without a doubt, Lucas' name will be mentioned. Another reminder that he's *gone* or *lost* is the last thing I could wish for.

"Wynter?"

My heart pounds loudly against my chest, my hands are still shaking from anger, and there's no end in sight for this waterfall of tears. Mum sighs heavily before her footsteps sound faint.

I stay confined within the four walls of my bedroom, refusing to leave, even though hunger is trying to convince me otherwise. My stomach makes all sorts of sounds, but leaving this room means facing reality. I can't even look Mum or Ara in the eye because anger starts to build up even though they've been nothing short of supportive. It's not them, it's me. Knowing that I'm the reason Lucas was out that evening hurts and suffocates every inch of me. Nothing in this entire world is important enough to warrant Lucas heading out so late to see me. He should have known that. Why didn't he know that? Why didn't I remind him that whatever it is, it can wait? That his safety matters more than anything, *anything*.

My body feels tense and there's no way to calm down. The keyboard sits there, reminding me of Lucas. Without hesitation, my pure rage takes over. I unplug the keyboard and move it abruptly into the cupboard along with the CD marked with my name, where they're both no longer in plain sight. Reminders of Lucas only adds to the wound that's embedded in my heart and mind. I face down all our photos together because seeing his perfectly formed dimples when he's no longer here is painful. He had the most genuine smile, and now no-one will ever see it again in person.

Laying in bed, I get my mobile phone out and replay the voicemail message I could never bring myself to delete:

Hey you, I knew you wouldn't answer because, of course, you hate phone calls. So I've got this prepared. I just wanted to say thank you for being you. A friend like you is hard to come by, but I'm glad that I gravitated to you back in Year 7! This is the first and last cheesy message you'll get, so hopefully it'll bring a smile to your face. I know you've been stressed about finding inspiration for your composition—here's your reminder that you inspire the people around you daily. Hopefully, we can do the same in return. See you at school. Lucas.

No matter how desperate I am to temporarily erase Lucas from my memory, if only to be able to lessen the numbing pain, deleting this voicemail would be a decision I'd instantly regret. So I hold onto his voice.

I wish I had answered that call.

9

The Final Verse

THERE'S A TRAY OF food outside my room. Mum and Ara have been taking turns bringing warm meals for me. Luckily it's the weekend, so I don't have to face the idea of going back to school yet. I don't know if I have the strength to muster it all up without Lucas.

One day at a time, I remind myself although instantly failing to believe so. The window blinds have been shut since Friday afternoon, so my eyes are yet to adjust to the sun's rays, struggling to sneak upon me. It's hard to face the day knowing an important part of you will never return.

Mr Knox, who lives next door, is an eighty-something-year-old who routinely mows his front lawn every Sunday morning, except for rainy days. Otherwise, he's there, whether it's a ten-degree Celsius day or forty. Ever since his wife Millie died, he's lived by following a strict schedule, day-in and day-out. I used to think it was a sad way to live life, especially living on your own. But in this very moment, I can feel a sense of togetherness that Mr Knox and I are somehow on the same wavelength even though we lost two different people in our lives.

He lost the kind some people spend a lifetime searching for. Their soulmate. Their one and only. Their forever. I've lost the kind some people spend a lifetime longing for. A true friend. Their best friend who isn't family. I wonder how I'll be spending my Sunday mornings. Because right now, I long for a routine of sleeping from sunup to sundown.

My composition notes scribbled on pieces of scrap paper sits across the room, on top of my disorganised study desk, wishing to out-stare me. It felt like it was only yesterday when my inspiration was beyond imaginable. It skyrocketed and for a brief moment, I felt like I could conquer the music task. That I would be able to finish the composition with weeks to spare for practise. Now, that inspiration has vanished along with the person who helped me find it in the first place.

I peer through my window, only adjusting the blinds slightly. Mr Knox is quick to notice the sudden movement and waves to me from afar. He gives the '*I know what you're going through*' nod before he continues with the lawn. I almost return the same gesture, a glimmer of expression other than torment, but the moment passes by too soon.

I hold my notes, with droplets of tears leaving marks on the pages. The melody doesn't ring the same way it did whilst writing it. The perfect notes strung together now feel as fragmented and shattered as the remaining pieces of my heart. Suddenly, every piano piece that plays is no longer just background music. It's significant. It's a reminder of what no longer is.

It's an undeniable, heart-provoking memory that can't be censored. It lays low, disguising itself in a seemingly beautiful tune, hitting number one on the music charts. But it's torture.

If Lucas and I had a melody, it wouldn't be perfect, but it would be imperfectly ours. Our melody began when we exchanged words for the first time, consciously aware that our actions would lead to a friendship that would grow and blossom from the familiarity and common ground of reading.

Verse one of our song was full of bus-stop conversations about *We Were Liars* and *To Kill a Mockingbird* and *Lord of the Flies* and *1984*. Sharing our innermost thoughts, whether our opinions were the same or not.

"How did you not see it coming?" Lucas questioned. "It was pretty obvious, especially towards the end that Cadence was the only survivor. You didn't catch the clues?"

"What clues?"

"For one thing, when Cadence sees them again at seventeen, they tell her how much she's changed since the last time they saw her, but she was surprised for the opposite reason—they hadn't changed at all."

"I guess while I was reading, I wasn't expecting to try and solve a mystery."

"Or maybe you read too fast," he jokes.

"Or maybe you read too slowly," I joke back.

I like that our opinions weren't always the same. We weren't trying to impress each other in all the wrong ways as most would at school. Of course, neither of us are offended by reading at different speeds. Some people read fast, often skimming through the text, whilst others read slowly, reading entire paragraphs word for word. I'm a bit of both. When I read novels, I tend to read faster, sometimes skipping a word or two. Textbooks though, I have to take my time reading, or nothing registers in my brain.

Verse one of our melody was perfect.

Verse two of our song felt more comfortable. We weren't afraid of being truthful with each other. We'd be more open about our feelings. It was as though a magnetic force tugged on our personalities. Some days I remember having to constantly do Box Breathing as Lucas would get on my nerves. It's a breathing method Mum taught me as she noticed my anxiety creeping up too often on the daily.

You breathe in through your nose, counting to four slowly, allowing yourself to feel the air enter your lungs. Then, you hold your breath for four seconds. This part took me a while to get used to as it always felt as though I was running out of oxygen as opposed to relaxing my body. Afterwards, you slowly exhale for another four seconds through your mouth. It works best if you do the entire method with your eyes closed, I guess to limit the distractions. You keep doing this until you feel yourself grounded again.

"Feeling better yet?" Lucas asks, halfway through my Box Breathing.

I try to ignore his voice because it interrupts the silence which helps with the breathing exercise.

"Almost?" Lucas asks only five seconds later, still halfway through my Box Breathing.

I pause and turn to face him so that he can clearly hear the words I'm about to say.

"You know when we're reading, and people think it's a smart idea to start a conversation, even though whatever it is they have to say isn't important? I mean, not important enough at least to interrupt our flow of words," I ask this with purpose.

"Yeah ..." Lucas responds, seeing where this lecture is headed to.

"Well, when I'm trying to do Box Breathing to re-centre myself, it doesn't really work effectively if someone is constantly talking to me during it."

"Why are you Box Breathing anyway? Is it proven to work? Why can't you just take normal deep breaths in and out?"

"Because ... Just because and you don't always need to know everything. Especially since you didn't care to tell me you already had plans to partner up with Leo for the Art project."

The sound of cockatoos fills the air. Lucas' complexion shines as bright as a freshly picked tomato disguising his tanned skin.

"I'm sorry ,Wynter. I just thought you'd maybe want to ..."

"You just thought. Assumed. Again."

If only Box Breathing was as effective now as it was then. This is when I need it to work the most and it hasn't left an impact, not even in the slightest.

Verse two of our song was about getting to know each other better, beyond reading. It didn't involve hitting notes in tune every single time, but it's what we needed to get to the chorus.

The chorus. This is when our words of affection turned into action. When our fireworks of anger, moments of disappointment, and days of heartache became a stronger bond for us two misfits. It's when we put each other's needs ahead of our own interest. When we truly believed that the friendship we shared is eternal and not a facade or a fire slowly burning.

"Are you sure you don't want me to call your mum? She's only a block away," Lucas asks as he helps me walk to the school nurse's office. *Limping isn't exactly how I pictured a Wednesday afternoon to look.*

"It's okay, there's nothing she can do to heal my wounded two left feet, not at this very second anyway."

"To be fair, you totally rocked it doing a double backflip like that."

We both laugh like hyenas.

"You mean, an accidental double backflip that I didn't know my body was capable of. This is why I hate P.E."

"Look at you now though, a limping ex-Olympian," Lucas teases, *although the thought of being an Olympian makes me laugh. I'm not horrible at sports, but I'm better coordinated at playing the keyboard.*

"The only true Olympian around here is you, Mr I'm-Not-Sporty-But-Can-Endure-The-Weight-Of-An-Injured-Olympian."

"An ex-Olympian," he corrects.

"In all honesty though," I say, *"thank you for being here for me, injured and all. It was so embarrassing doing what I did, but you quickly rescued me from that horrifying situation."*

"Like a true hero!" He tries flexing his 'guns' and the sight of this makes us both cry from laughter.*

I hate that I can no longer put your needs ahead of my own. I hate that no matter how hard I try, there would be no point because your existence has left this world.

The chorus of our song I would play on repeat, if I could.

The final verse. It hit me like the first day of winter. When the windows frost instantly without warning, and you wake up with hair reaching for the sky that crawls on your skin. Just as mine and Lucas' walls fell and our friendship was unbreakable. Every beat of this verse, Lucas wasn't around to witness. Once the brightest star in my galaxy, now destroyed. The final verse hurts. I grasp for fresh air, I try Box Breathing, I try anything to breathe normally again. Lucas, you left me too soon. You were only sixteen.

And now I face the remainder of our melody with lingering, bittersweet reminders of you. The limited days we shared, torments me in the form of every lyric, of every line, of every song. It creeps upon me, aiming for my far-from-healing heart.

On the radio, music at the shops, a band strumming a beat at the café, and old tunes on my ancient MP3 player. *Anywhere* music is played, there you'll be. This terrifying thought makes it hard for me to leave my room. It's during these brief but very real moments I know will happen, where there's no escape from the reality of your disappearance, where my heart will crumble instead of restore. The gut-wrenching truth that with every new adventure that awaits me, big or small, it *only* awaits me without you by my side.

The final verse of our melody is agony.

No matter how many times our melody is played, the final verse still blindsides me every time. Lucas, why did you have to leave before we got to the bridge of the melody? Where it would have been days of back-to-back adventures and never-ending laughter. The kind that makes our bellies hurt.

The bridge of our melody is left untold.

10

Reality

MONDAY MORNING COMES AROUND as quickly as Sunday ends. Mum left a note and slid it under my bedroom door last night: *If you're not ready for school, it's okay. There's no pressure to go back soon. But please, try to get some fresh air. Love you, Mum.*

What even is fresh air? There's so much pollution, I'd have to travel thousands of kilometres away from home just to find the first check-point of 'fresh air' and that would probably take hours of travelling by any moving vehicle.

Although dark circles are marked under my eyes, and my skin is as dry as sandpaper, I make a conscious effort to rise from the comfort of my bed.

I am braver than I think, stronger than I feel. I have the courage to face my fears.

If affirmations really work, today will be a test for that. Maybe by some odd miracle, the last couple of days have been one big lie—a reality show where toying with peoples' emotions attracts viewers. If I go to school, then maybe the anger will go away. It will be a good distraction. I need that.

***

I enter the school gates and my surroundings surprise me. What happened to the sorry eyes? Everyone is going about their morning as though there isn't one less student, forever.

I see Stacey hop off a bus in my peripheral view with a mission to catch up to me. Although I notice this, I don't entirely slow down but that isn't an issue for Stacey because it seems she's the true Olympian around here.

Without any shortness of breath, Stacey is besides me in a flash.

"Hey, Wynter."

"Hey."

"I'm sorry I wasn't there for you on Friday, my parents kept me home. They were worried that, y'know ..."

"They'd lose you too." I finish Stacey's sentence because even though we haven't known each other for that long, her thoughts are somewhat predictable because they're similar to my own.

Stacey nods. When I look at her though, I'm expecting a blank expression like everyone else, but her face speaks differently. Her downcast eyes reveal sorrow. Deep pain.

The silence is deafening. Today was supposed to feel like 'back to reality' so that I can prove to myself that losing Lucas doesn't mean life doesn't carry on. I mean, everyone around me has already proven that idea with their smiling faces and disregard for the Friday that had just passed.

"Are you okay, Stacey?" Something's hiding behind her visage of composure.

"Me? I should be asking you that. I really wanted to be there for you. I mean, even now. It's only been a few days. To be honest, I wasn't expecting you to be at school today. Are you holding up okay?" Stacey's eyes jitter and avoid direct contact with mine.

"I'm supposed to be okay, right? Like everyone else here today. Back to reality."

"Lucas *is* your reality, Wynter. Don't forget that, yeah?"

"I just want to go a day without thinking of him. To make the pain lessen. I thought school could do that."

"Cut yourself some slack. You don't need to put up a strong front. He only died a few days ago … *Your* own heart only broke a few days ago. Let it heal, Wynter. It's what Lucas would have wanted."

"How do you know what Lucas would have wanted?" The question rolls off my tongue too quickly.

Stacey pauses, attempting to construct a reply and to her relief, she's saved by the bell.

"I'll see you at recess?" she confirms. I nod *yes* and walk the opposite way.

Questions flood my mind as I make my way to Homeroom. Do Stacey and Lucas know each other long before she started school here? Lucas seemed to give the impression that he knew Stacey beyond her name. It makes sense if they do because that would explain the despair hiding behind Stacey's weepy eyes. Maybe she lost a friend that day too. Whilst plausible, this thought triggers annoyance. Do I know my best friend the way I thought I did? *I'm missing something.*

"Wynter, how are you?" Mr Finn pulls me aside with a concerned demeanour.

"I'm well," I reply, wanting to end the conversation before it escalates to words I'm trying to avoid hearing today.

"If you need someone to talk to, the school counsellor is in today. Miss Xi will be in all week. She's confirmed you're welcome to swing by her office anytime."

"Okay."

His words catch me off-guard. It's unusual for him to appear empathetic. Mr Finn has had a 'strict' teacher reputation throughout the years. Mum says that he's the complete opposite to her and admits that she often has to bite her tongue when they cross paths, especially in the staff room.

Whilst Mum tries to have a balanced view on everything, Mr Finn is a prime example of a massively skewed and tilted scale. It's either his way or no way at all. Mum says it would have been nice if he showed more of his 'caring' side because a lot of the boys might then find a teacher they can confide in. Especially for those misunderstood at home, or with parents of high academic expectations and continuously fail to meet their pristine standards. As much as Mum tries to connect with them, it doesn't take a genius to recognise that it would be easier for these boys to approach a male teacher as a father figure. That isn't really an option at the moment though.

Drama class is first period today. Mrs Yieldeman is on leave for the next two weeks. Mum says Lucas' death affected her more than anyone could have known. Mrs Yieldeman is a middle-aged vibrant, happy-go-lucky woman, but deep down, hidden amongst all her masks of happiness, is a grieving mother.

Kelsie was only two months old when she died in her sleep. Mrs Yieldeman's whole world turned upside-down and even though Kelsie died over fifteen years ago, it still breaks her heart daily. She would have been close in age to me.

"It took her years to move on," Mum explained. "And even then, Kelsie is forever in her heart. Always."

Now I notice the little things Mrs Yieldeman does throughout class, which just never crossed my mind before. Occasionally she'll pause by the blackboard, mid-sentence, to take several deep breaths. Other times, whilst at her desk, she'll close her eyes momentarily, with a different gaze upon opening them. One time Ali thought it would be funny to tease her about being an old childless woman. Mrs Yieldeman spent the rest of that period 'looking for something' in the storeroom. If only I knew at the time, I would have tried to be a source of comfort, even for a short while.

Our substitute teacher walks in, quite timid. She looks like she's in her early twenties straight out of university.

"Good morning, everyone. My name is Miss Jansen and I'll be relieving Mrs Yieldeman until she returns. Today we're continuing off from the last lesson's task. If you can get into your groups, please."

Of course, I'm grouped with Ali. The chances of that happening are high if past statistics were to prove my point correctly. It's as though Ali's sole purpose in life is to be two steps ahead of me. To hover over me like a lingering headache.

"I'll make my way around each group, checking on your progress."

The class agrees and flees to their pre-arranged groups.

Ali clears her throat and starts pointing with her pink manicured nail. "Okay, so to make this work we need a scribe, that can be you, Zoe, your handwriting is the easiest to read. Then, Violet, Stacey and Alex can be the actors. I'll be the narrator, obviously. Okay, let's get started."

Stacey calls Ali out, "We haven't assigned a role for Wynter yet."

"Oh," Ali responds, with no regret in her tone. "I assumed she's unfit for this task. Okay now, everyone get into your—"

"What's wrong with you, Ali? Are you purposely trying to treat Wynter like hell or are you just a naturally bad person?" Stacey's rage shocks us all.

"It's okay, Stacey, it's not worth it," I say in a low tone, with an amateur attempt to move Stacey away from Ali.

Ali looks me straight in the eye. "Oh, how cute. You've replaced your dead best friend with another piece of trash."

I close my eyes and ignore her words, determined to drown them out as background noise.

"What? You can't accept reality?" Ali continues, with a smirk stamped across her face.

Again, I remain calm and collected.

"Seriously? You want to keep acting like you'll still see Lucas today?" Ali laughs.

I wait for everyone to laugh along with Ali, but as the longest seconds pass by, I notice that Ali's the only one laughing this time.

Ali nudges me. "Hello?" she continues. "Remember Lucas, your *dead* friend?"

Today was supposed to feel normal but nothing about the last hour alone does. Ali has crossed the line and every nerve in my body is resisting to respond physically. As I'm about to walk away, Stacey grabs me and pulls me back. She knows I need to do this for me. For Lucas. For everyone who Ali has ever hurt.

So instead, I don't hold back with words. The overwhelming mixed emotions burst at the seams of my patience. Ali's been getting away with hurting others for too long. It needs to stop. I don't have time to construct a carefully thought out reply. The rage brewing inside me takes over. This has never happened in the whole sixteen years of my life.

"You can make fun of me all you like. You want to scream out *red* at the top of your lungs? Go for your life. Throw all your wasted sandwiches on me. Trip me over a thousand times more. You can even turn the entire school against me. I don't care. Just don't ever, *ever* speak of Lucas like that. That trash you speak of is worth way more than you and your fake circle of friends. Lucas was *real*. He was the realest person to step foot into this school. He was kind and genuinely cared about others. He stood by me when I had no-one. When I had to start high school alone because *you* ditched our friendship for the cool crowd. I don't know, are you enjoying the ride up high on your pedestal? You call him trash? Then all of us, right here, right now, we must be lower than dirt! You stand there thinking you're better than everyone else? I actually feel sorry for you. If you only knew how it feels like to have a real friend, even just one. But you never will. You call Lea and Ivy your friends? They're just your followers, waiting for the day to share your limelight. If you had that one friend you cared so deeply about, you'd know that painstaking feeling if they were to ever slip away from you, forever. The pain of opening your eyes each morning knowing you won't ever see them again. That you can only hold onto that one damn voicemail just to hear their voice. If you only knew. You have no right to even whisper his name. You don't deserve to speak about *my* dead best friend. And leave Stacey alone."

Overcome with anger, I storm out of the room with no clear destination in mind. I don't care, even if it means I get suspended. I'm running and crying and stumbling and shaking. Until I run into the arms that are there to catch me before I fall. Every time.

Mum.

11

Five Senses

A RA DOESN'T STAY BACK for debate practice. She'll still ace it when they compete against other schools because she has a natural ability to talk her way through any topic under the sun. I think the majority of it comes from self-confidence because she can make anything sound believable and factual. It wouldn't surprise me though if she occasionally sneaks in a made-up fact.

Usually, Ara stays back long enough to avoid catching the bus home. Mum finishes by then so they drive home together. After Dad's accident, it took Mum several years before she gained the courage to drive again, so I spent most of my newborn stage being pushed in a pram to and from places. Aunt Marge kept Mum grounded on days she felt it was all too much. A day didn't go by without them talking on the phone. If only she didn't live so far away, oceans apart, then she would have been Mum's personal sidekick in real-time.

When Mum and Ara arrive home, they find me cocooned in a fleece blanket, laying across the couch. They're both standing in my direct view, but my body feels lifeless. It's begging for me to spend the next few years in hibernation even though my nose inhales one of my favourite smells—a smell I could devour in one bite. But I remain stationary. My heart beats a continuous thump that feels so intense, Mum and Ara can probably hear the beat from where they're standing.

"Hey, Wynter, we got some takeaway on the way home. Hot chips and gravy."

They glance my way with hopeful but desperate pleas in the disguise of smiles.

I want to reply, 'Maybe next time.' But the strength to respond is exhausting before I've even tried. Their hopeful smiles even out.

There's a cloud looming over my head, building up so much rain, without any indication as to when it will pour. The forecast doesn't seem too promising. As I glimpse through the open window, the sun is slowly setting in chunks of reds and bright oranges, a sight I'd normally find picturesque. But not today.

A soccer ball glides over the fence and bounces into a water-filled pothole, causing a huge splatter of muddy water to spray onto Mum's thriving garden bed. This yanks my heart out and causes the pit of my stomach to twist into knots of pain. A sinking pain that I can't reel in. That one splash spirals my mind to face a memory of Lucas and his love for the rain.

Lucas would talk about the weather with so much passion the same way a Musician talks about their songs and the inspiration behind them. It's funny because they say that when you're in a situation where you're stuck talking to someone you have no common ground with, you end up talking about the weather and that's as far as the conversation goes. But with Lucas, you could talk about the weather for hours on end and you'd walk away feeling refreshed afterwards, even if the forecast looked grim.

"Argh, looks like it'll be raining this afternoon," I complain, knowing that I'll have to trek home and my socks will be drenched along the way, which is never a comfortable feeling. Whilst home is only a two-minute walk from the bus stop, it's still two whole minutes of getting soaked. My umbrella sits uselessly by our front porch.

"Gotta love the rain," Lucas remarks.

"You love any weather, to be fair."

"Try putting aside your preconceived ideas about the horrible, dreaded rain and you may just find that it's really calming."

"It's only calming when you're at home, indoors, curled up in bed reading a book. But when you have to walk in it … without an umbrella?" I say, testing whether 'love' is the right word to use in the same sentence as 'rain'.

"Dad taught me this thing when I was six years old and it's always stuck. So we've got our five senses, right?"

"Right … go on."

"The more we use them consciously, the more we appreciate things that we may have otherwise looked at differently."

"You mean, annoyingly … like walking in the rain."

"Yeah, it just takes practice until it becomes a habit. With that scenario, first I'd look with my eyes. Have you ever just stopped and taken in how mesmerising raindrops actually are?"

"You have a point there. Keep going …"

"And then I listen. Just take in the pitter-patter sounds. Hear it play a rhythmic tune. You'd be surprised how soothing it can be. Kinda like when we play the piano. Just think of the raindrops as keys dropping a note."

"And then you taste the rain?" I joke, although genuinely curious now as to how he'd use our sense of taste in this case.

"You got me there. But even then, if you can't physically use that sense in whatever scenario, you can still find a way to apply it. Like picturing a pigeon drinking the fallen rainwater from a puddle or fountain, and how that must feel like for them."

"You're something else," I tell him, making sure he knows he has a weird but wonderful brain.

"And even though rain itself has no scent, it leaves behind a fresh, somewhat earthy smell. Maybe you should try your Box Breathing out in the rain one time. You'll inhale the musky trails of it then."

"I have to admit, you're pretty persuasive."

"And don't forget to feel the rain, which you obviously will because you're umbrella-less. But actually allow yourself to feel how amazing raindrops are. They literally fall from the sky. That droplet of rain that lands on your arm, it fell from thousands of kilometres away," he adds.

"Well, when you say it like that ... You have a way of making something so mundane sound so incredible."

"So it looks like we'll have an incredible walk home this arvo then, right?"

"In the rain," I say, smiling.

Hopping off the bus later that afternoon, the rain sprinkled us with a big hello.

"Look at you," Lucas teases, "walking in the rain and all."

And along with that remark, Lucas swings his foot, kicking a puddle which splashes onto us both. His dimples pop as he sees the look on my face, clearly obvious that it's the first time I've been this drenched in the rain.

I let out a playful scream and take aim at another puddle, as though I'm about to kick a soccer ball for the winning point, until Lucas is just as drenched.

We stand side by side, with our clothes sticking onto our skin, not a single dry patch in sight. And yet we smile. We laugh. We take in this moment.

Lucas takes hold of my hand and twirls me around like a ballerina in a music box. We start swaying carelessly, following each other's lead as we dance and glide across the puddles. Our very own stage. Our two left feet are in sync. So are our hearts. To the crisp crunch of the autumn leaves beneath us. To the raindrops forming as a beautiful backdrop. We dance. Without a single worry in our minds.

I continue laying cocooned, wondering whether I'll be like *The Very Hungry Caterpillar* and at the end of all this, I'll spread my wings like a beautiful butterfly, fluttering freely away from the dark clouds. It seems far-fetched because every piece of work feels like a challenge right now. Switching the T.V. on is a miniscule but impossible task. And hot chips with gravy? My absolute favourite, especially on a cold and miserable day like today. But I can't bring myself to budge with any form of excitement about it. Movement is draining.

"We'll be in the kitchen if you need anything. I was thinking we could order some pizza for dinner tonight?" Mum suggests, aware that pizza is another one of my favourites. Two take-outs in one day, that's unheard of in this household. I'm grateful for Mum's efforts in trying to make me feel better, but I don't want to break it to her that I just need some quiet. I don't know how a heart is programmed to heal, but both my heart and mind need to work together because right now, all five senses are failing to recognise anything but pain.

I see pain.

I hear pain.

I taste pain.

I smell pain.

And I feel pain.

Lucas would be able to turn this heartache around—the master of cultivating your senses. But he's not around anymore to help with that.

Mum acknowledges my silence and treads quietly into the kitchen with Ara following behind. They give me the space I need even though it breaks their hearts that this is the best outcome they can get from me.

When the coast is clear, I stretch my legs in an attempt to reverse my pins and needles. I unwrap myself from the cocoon I've become comfortable in, although I'm barely ready to take flight. In a trance-like state, I walk across the room to make the giant trek to my bedroom. I'm stopped mid-way by the sight of Mum's treasured Thai Constellation looking greener and healthier than ever before. For a brief second I convince myself that it can ignite a joy in me the same way it does for Mum. There's a new leaf unfurling so delicately with beautiful streaks of white. I admire it for a short while but its presence doesn't heal me. I'm no better than I was thirty seconds ago.

When I reach the finish line and close my bedroom door, I let out a sigh of relief. To be in my own privacy where I can fill the entire space with tears and no-one would have to know. To keep my emotions from being on full display.

The calendar is in full view, forcing me to face the reality that I can't avoid, which means completing my assignments and the dreaded music task. They're all clearly marked, with their due dates nearing. Whilst my teachers have been more than lenient and understanding, allowing me some extra time to complete my work, I know that this can't continue for the rest of the year. How can I move forward if I let these exceptions be okay?

There's a soft knock on my door, interrupting my chain of thoughts. The calmness in each tap means it's Mum.

"Wynter ... I know you need some space, but I just wanted to let you know that I know about what happened in class. I just got off the phone with Mrs Yieldeman."

My mind has been so off-guard that I completely forgot about that. I never quite explained to Mum what actually happened. She was there to catch me from a fall. To comfort me. She didn't need a reason. She never asked. Normally I'd share every single detail with her in a heartbeat, but my heart was torn. Right now it still feels too torn to reply.

"Miss Jansen updated your teacher on everything, sweetie. About Ali harassing you ... About ..."

Mum pauses and I hold my breath waiting to hear the rest.

"If teaching Ali for the last four years has taught me a thing or two, I know that your reaction was from your limits being pushed. Trust me, sweetie, she pushes my limits too. I just have to hold it together more because I'm her teacher."

I want nothing else but to open the door and hug Mum tightly. But the numbing feeling travelling through my hands and feet keeps me from moving.

"Ali was sent to Mr Lee's office and he explained what happened to her parents. To his surprise, Ali's parents asked her to say an apology."

Wow, I think to myself. Ali's parents are known to get her out of whatever messy situation she's gotten herself into. She's always had victims apologise, just like Arti. It's never been the other way around. Ali apologising to Mr Lee sounds like a different Ali was in that office.

"And Wynter, sweetie, you'll be pleased to know that Mrs Yieldeman has rearranged the class performance groups so that you're no longer with Ali. She happily moved Stacey as well to be in yours."

When I hear Mum leave, I sift through the pile of paper on my desk. Just as I'm about to figure out whether to tackle the assignments or continue to hibernate, the doorbell chimes, echoing up the staircase walls.

"I'll see if she's feeling okay for some company," I hear Mum say, but I can't quite hear the reply from the person on the other side of the door.

Mum must have instructed Ara to check on me because it's Ara who knocks on my door.

"There's someone here to see you," she says from behind the door. My door isn't locked, but Ara is pretty switched on when it comes to knowing boundaries and when a good or bad time is to make her presence known. She knows that abruptly entering my room would be an invasion of my privacy, even if all I'm doing is sitting by my desk. She tried once and it went horribly wrong. She learnt the hard way.

I clear my throat, swallowing deeply. "Who?" I'm practically whispering, but I manage to speak.

Opening the door slowly, I find Ara standing there appearing unsure whether to greet me with a smile, a frown, or to look away.

Before she can answer, I peer down the spiral staircase and without needing to hear his voice, I know right away who it is. Looks like I'm using my sense of sight effectively right now. Lucas would be proud. Possibly.

Guy stands still with both hands sitting snug in the pockets of his jeans. If he was a tad shorter, it would seem as though Lucas himself, in the flesh, was the person standing in my view. I can only see half of his face from this angle, but it's enough to open the floodgate of tears. It breaks me into a million pieces not because he reminds me of Lucas, but because he reminds me of how Lucas looks. I know it sounds crazy because it hasn't been very long at all since Lucas' death, but it just hit me how quickly his features have started to fade away in my memory. I feel guilt spreading throughout my veins and a promise slipping away from my very own hands. The promise to never allow Lucas' face and voice to ever fade. Lucas' whole being should still be crystal clear, but why can't I remember every minuscule feature that made him, him?

"He came to see you," Ara says. "I'll let him know if you're not—"

"It's okay," I interrupt.

I collect my thoughts and gather myself as though I'm a puzzle of 1000 pieces being assembled on fast-forward. As I Box Breathe, I release nerves along with my exhales. *It will be fine,* I pep talk to myself.

I'm still in my pyjamas, which I'd normally feel embarrassed about still wearing past noon, but I don't feel the need to get changed into clothing that makes me appear as though I've got everything together. There are still missing pieces to my puzzle, there's no hiding that.

As my foot takes one small step onto the staircase, I suddenly feel all the nerves re-entering my system. I hold onto the railing, allowing it to support the dead weight my wobbly legs are trying to hold.

Guy sees me instantly and shoots a half-smile. It's still friendly and warm, just like Lucas', but with less life and happiness. I can't blame him for that. As soon as my feet land on the last step, Guy leans in for a hug, caressing me in a way that shows he needed this comfort much more. Although he and Lucas are each other's doppelgängers, Guy is the more sentimental and affectionate one. He'll hug anyone who needs a little extra T.L.C. and is never afraid to wear his heart on his sleeve. Lucas on the other hand, whilst he's just as friendly, shows it more through his words. His reminders. His natural calming aura.

"Hi, Wynter. I'm sorry to drop in like this. I probably should have messaged first."

"It's okay. If I'm not at school, I'm just here anyway."

It feels strange to hear Guy's voice. It makes me miss Lucas that much more. Not only do they look alike, but they sound alike too. On the phone, you wouldn't be able to tell them apart.

"How are you?" he asks with genuine care in his eyes.

"I could be better. But I'm out of bed today. How 'bout you? And your parents?"

He breathes deeply. "We're all out of bed today now, too. Mum's struggling, but she's got Dad and I to help her. One day at a time, I guess."

I knew that hug was more than just a hug. There's no-one to support Guy through all of this. He's being strong for his parents, but he lost a brother too. He needs reassurance right now like a small child needs constant reminders from their parents.

"I found this in Lucas' room. He was halfway through writing it. He didn't quite get to finish it."

Guy hands me an A4 sheet of paper folded neatly in half.

"A few nights before the accident, he told me how you would read his mind, unknowingly. How only you ever could, no-one else."

As I unfold the paper, my heart instantly aches. *Dear Wynter.* Beneath the heading are lines of musical notes and lyrics. Some words are crossed out and replaced by a better word or key. Lucas had been writing a song dedicated to me for his music performance. *Moonlight Sonata* was a cover-up.

"Since you're the only person who can read his mind ... Maybe you could finish writing it."

It takes me several minutes just staring blankly at the page. His handwriting is so messy, you'd think he was destined to be a Doctor, but it somehow adds to the beauty of the composition. It has his unique imprint on it. Reading the first several lines makes me choke up. It's written so perfectly despite the imperfect script:

Dear Wynter,
You're the words floating on this page,
You're every note forming this tune.

Guy notices how having this in my hands pains me deeply. It's a mixed pain. The kind where it's such a delightful surprise that it hurts to not have known about it while Lucas was still alive. To be able to see him play, hear him sing, and read the rest of his thoughts that he wasn't able to put down on paper.

"Life's just like this song," I say whilst still avoiding direct eye contact. "It just ends. There's no way of knowing for certain when it'll happen. It'll end, mid-sentence. Mid-breath. Mid-anything. And then you're left with an incomplete piece of their life."

"You inspired Lucas to write music. Please, keep this."

"Thank you," I whisper, almost inaudibly. I swallow deeply and resist crying. My eyes are already sore and puffy from all the tears I've shed. The paper sits close to my chest. Hugging it tightly, it's the closest feeling I'll get to hugging Lucas in reality.

Dear Lucas,
You're the words buried in my heart,
You're every underrated perfect piece of art.
A wave of emotions, captivating and real.

12

Superpower

Miss Xi's office is cosy. There's a small poster above her desk that says, *I counsel, what's your superpower?* Clever. Straight away it shifts my brain into thinking of my superpower instead of anxiously waiting for Miss Xi to arrive and endure all the questions she'll be asking.

When I was six years old, my Kindergarten teacher asked the class, "If you had a superpower, what would it be?" My answer was *invisibility*. Looking back, it's funny how life plays out because I was practically invisible throughout the years that followed in school. Ali's superpower was to be able to fly. During recess, she would stand on top of a tree stump and pretend to fly as she jumped off. One time she flew towards me, pretending to save me from the bad guys, and that's how our friendship started. Ali became my best friend, and she'd be the voice I needed when mine failed. She was the only one who saw me as a visible being, and it felt nice while it lasted.

I ponder about what my superpower would be now. Maybe if I change it from invisibility to something else, it will become a reality. I laugh at that thought, knowing how ludicrous it is.

"Hello, Wynter. Would you like a warm tea or hot chocolate to drink?"

Miss Xi enters the room and walks to a drinks station she has set up by the back corner of the room. It's like a mini trendy café. There's another poster strategically placed above it that says: *Love is in the air, and it smells like coffee.*

The aroma of freshly grounded coffee beans that Miss Xi prepares for herself somehow triggers happy memories of Lucas. Like the time when we thought we would order a cappuccino, only to realise although we love the smell of coffee, it left a bitter taste that our taste buds weren't ready for yet. We were fourteen years old. Lucas ended up drinking the rest because it was a waste of $3.50, whereas my stomach couldn't handle another sip.

"No, but thanks," I reply, just in case I'm served a tea or hot chocolate that I won't be able to finish. I'll feel bad giving back a cup that isn't empty.

Miss Xi accepts my answer without breaking free from her warm glance. There's something about her friendly nature that intertwines a feeling of both happiness and confidence. She returns to her seat with a hot cup hugged between her hands.

"I hope you don't mind, I missed my morning coffee today."

"All good," I say. "I love the smell of coffee. Not so much the taste though. Lucas and I ..." I stop before I complete the sentence, realising I had mentioned his name so casually.

"It's okay, Wynter, go on."

"It's just that, Lucas and I once tried coffee. We often wondered why adults loved it so much. We ordered two cappuccinos only to discover neither of us liked it."

"It's good to hold onto these memories."

"I guess so ..."

"I know things have been hard for you, Wynter. Especially this past week. It's brave of you to chat with me today."

"I'm not sure I'm brave. I feel far from it."

"Small steps, Wynter. One step at a time. No-one's expecting you to take giant leaps."

"It feels like everyone's taking leaps, except for me."

"Can you tell me about what happened on that day?"

"The day I found out? It was too late."

"Too late?"

"It just was ..."

Miss Xi's eyes are fixated on mine. It doesn't feel intimidating, just kind and gentle.

"It's okay if you don't want to share everything today, Wynter."

I pull out the CD from my backpack and hand it to her without an explanation.

"Is this from Lucas?" Miss Xi tries to fill in the blanks.

A nod is all I can manage in response.

"Wynter, the circumstances were out of your control. It was out of his as well. Sadly, it was a tragic accident that no-one could have seen coming. Does this CD mean anything important to you?"

I shrug.

"Would you like me to play it?"

"I don't know."

Miss Xi moves to sit besides me instead. "What's on this CD, Wynter?"

"If it wasn't for this CD, Lucas wouldn't have been outside."

"I see," Miss Xi responds, realising the value this CD holds. The blank spaces are now slowly being filled.

"Lucas wouldn't have been on his way to mine. He wouldn't have crossed paths with that reckless driver. I can't help but blame myself." I'm surprised by my response. Something about Miss Xi makes it a little easier to open up, even if all my replies might indicate otherwise.

"What you're feeling is a normal part of grieving. But what happened isn't your fault. Remember that. Have you played the CD?"

"No. I can't bring myself to come to know whatever it is that took his life away. I can't bring myself to throw it out either."

"When you're ready, I think it will be a good idea for you to play it. You're holding onto fear, but it might be the opposite of that. It may be the weight lifted from your shoulders that you need."

I sit in silence, fumbling with my fingers, unsure how to respond to that.

"Whilst it's a good idea, Wynter, just remember there's no rush. When you're ready, you'll know." Miss Xi passes me the CD, ensuring it's in my hands safely.

"When did you realise counselling was your superpower?" I ask. Perhaps it's out of line, but the words spring out of my mouth without warning.

"I never knew I had a superpower until it was pointed out to me. Sometimes it takes a fresh set of eyes to see you for who you truly are, or what you can become. I've always had the need to help others, but I wasn't always an excellent listener. One day, my best friend was crying because she had lost a new Walkman her parents gifted her, and I listened to her worries. For the first time, I didn't talk over someone halfway through their sentence. Being able to actively listen, it changed the way I viewed people in need. Sometimes, all they need is for someone to hear them."

"That's really nice. Are you still best friends?"

"Twenty years of friendship, even though she's moved to the other end of the globe. We still take the time to visit each other every year though. Thank goodness for the Internet, otherwise, we'd be waiting weeks on end for mail to land in our post boxes."

"Lucas is being cremated this Saturday. I don't know if I'm strong enough to attend the funeral service afterwards."

"There won't be a dry eye in the room, don't hold back your tears. You won't be alone, Wynter. I'm sure his family will be grateful to see you there, too."

I nod, trying to cover up my fears. Attending his funeral will make his death feel official. As though it's the final puzzle piece before moving on to the next set. I'm not ready to move on. I feel guilty that I have a choice in that.

"Thank you for listening, Miss Xi. I appreciate it."

"How about we continue this conversation tomorrow? Same time? You'll get through this, Wynter. I promise."

Leaving her office, my heart is heavy, but thankful. Somehow, the session felt more liberating than it did terrifying. The nerves that envelops me slowly eases, squeezing in a positive thought for the day ahead.

I am braver than I think, stronger than I feel. I have the courage to face my fears.

Walking towards Art class, Ali brushes past my shoulder, but by the shocked expression on her face, she didn't realise it was me.

"Wynter, I, uh ..."

My body freezes with the sudden realisation that Ali is speechless. The only other time I've witnessed Ali lost for words was in Year 6 when she wasn't selected as School Captain. She was certain she had it in the bag. When the school principal announced Clara's name, Ali's mouth dropped to the ground, and her body was as still as a statue. It took away from Clara's moment.

This time seems different. Her stillness isn't that of annoyance or suppressed anger.

"It's okay." I shrug it off and carry on.

"Wait—"

Ali holds my arm, stopping me in my tracks. Her eyes are pleading for me to listen, they appear vulnerable. I stand quietly, giving her the moment she needs. Just as Ali opens her mouth to speak, Lea and Ivy approach us from a nearby block.

"There you are! We've been looking all over the school for you," Ivy says, relieved that their long-lost Queenbee has been found.

"Um ... What's up with her?" Lea says as she looks at me in disgust. I mean, how dare I be within the vicinity of Ali, right? Even though Ali approached me.

Ali looks at me and then quickly turns away. Her demeanour changed within a split second of Lea and Ivy arriving. They link arms as they head off to class. Ali turns slightly, glancing my way. For a short-lived moment, I'm reminded of Ali from when she was the dependable, self-sacrificing best friend many moons ago.

As I turn the corner, Stacey greets me and links arms. I've never been the type to link arms, I don't understand the purpose of it, but it seems to be a thing around this school. We head off to P.E. together. Stacey is pumped for the Beep Test, which I'm of course dreading. Apparently, Stacey was the last one standing at her old school back in the U.S. every year.

Lucas and I made a conscious effort to try our best, but our best could barely get us to a level 5. Again, we're not athletic in any way. This flashback of Lucas surprisingly brings a smile to my face. If Lucas were here, he'd be cheering me on to get past level 5. We made it a goal to at least attempt a 5.4—it's the level required by police officers. We're not entirely sure how true that fact is, but it's what Martin told the whole class last year because his dad is a cop.

"You'll be fine," Stacey reassures me. "Plus, it's just a random test anyway. All about endurance more than skill."

"Easy for you to say, you're basically a future Olympian."

We share a giggle and I feel happy. A smile almost drops.

Mr Wilson instructs us to line up and spread out to allow us some running space. He has the Beep Test ready to play from an old cassette player.

Beep.

It begins.

When my pace slows down and my legs start to feel like jelly, it's a level 5.2. Not quite the police officer passing mark Lucas and I had hoped for, but hey, it's an improvement from last year's result.

As I sit by the sideline, I wonder whether Lucas would have exceeded a 5.4. Stacey's still going, without breaking a sweat.

I miss you, Lucas, especially during times like this. My Beep Test sideline buddy.

13

Hot Chocolate

Miss Xi helps herself to a cup of hot chocolate this time.

"Are you sure you don't want one? I make great hot chocolate."

"I'm a really slow drinker, I might not finish it in time for next period."

"We can drink slowly together, then."

Miss Xi's cheeks curve, beaming in pleasure as she stirs me a cup of hot chocolate. It warms my heart and reminds me that you don't have to do grand gestures to make someone's day. Sometimes all you need is to share a warm beverage.

"My nephews love it when I make them some. They say Aunt Lily's is the best."

I take a sip, and it instantly travels down my throat and my insides are filled with happiness. It sure is delicious.

"I can see why. This tastes great. Thank you."

"You're welcome, it's my pleasure."

"I've been thinking about what you said yesterday. About playing the CD."

Miss Xi gently places her mug on the desk and then leans forward to listen intently.

"Go on, Wynter. It's okay."

"A part of me is still holding on to the *why's* and it's a stab to the wound thinking about how this piece of plastic could end someone's life. If I knew he wanted to show me right away, maybe I could have been the one riding my bike to him instead. That way history would look different."

"We can't predict the future and we can't change the past. Remember, it's not your fault, Wynter. Unfortunately, sometimes people are just in the wrong place, at the wrong time, and that's exactly what happened with Lucas. An unfortunate event. Do you think Lucas would want you to play the CD still?"

"He would have probably put it in the CD player himself."

"It can be scary facing our fears. After all, they're a fear for a reason. Let me show you something."

Miss Xi takes a mobile phone out of her handbag.

"This is the last message I received from my mother before she passed away from ovarian cancer. The night before her death, I had visited her in hospital and we had a disagreement because she wanted me to accept that she was dying and that would mean I'd be living on my own because my father was never in the picture. The thought of living without her made me angry. You see, I wasn't angry at *her*, I was angry at the circumstances. But I let my anger out on her. I was only nineteen at the time. I wish I had known better. Now, listen to this."

Miss Xi plays the voicemail message:

"Lily, darling, I don't have long to go I'm afraid. Dr Patel has a sorry look in his eyes each time he drops by for my regular checks. I'm sorry for

leaving you behind like this. I wish my body was stronger. Please darling, I long to hear your voice, just one last time before I go. I love you."

Miss Xi wipes a lone teardrop from her cheek. "I never called her back."

"I'm so sorry, Miss Xi."

"No, it's okay. It's my load to carry. I wanted you to listen to this, because for many years I built up anger, regret and pain. I was angry at myself for not being there for my mother's last breath. I wish I had called her back to reassure her I'd be by her bedside through it all. I wish I could have said 'I love you too' but it was too late."

My eyes are watery, understanding how hard it is for Miss Xi to share her story.

"It wasn't until I let go of the guilt that I carried for all those years, that I could live life again ... Actually live and not drown in my sorrows. Live life the way my mother would have wanted me to. Deep in my heart, I know she has forgiven me and wouldn't want me to walk through life with a heavy heart. This is why I knew it was my purpose in life to be a grief counsellor. Hopefully, I can help others going through the same heartache and pain because I only had myself to lean on when I desperately needed a pair of listening ears."

"I wish I could be brave. I tell myself every morning that I'm braver than I think. But it's hard to believe those words when the truth is I'm afraid."

"Being brave doesn't mean forgetting Lucas' existence. I still play that voicemail message every day just to hear my mother's voice, no matter how painful the memory attached to it is. Try seeing yourself the way Lucas would have. Even the way Ara and Mrs Hope do. You're brave, Wynter. Extremely brave. Do you think playing the CD will help lessen the load you're carrying?"

"I'm afraid of the unknown. But, Lucas would have told me it's okay and not to dwell on the *what if's*. He somehow had the right words to say, even though he never realised that about himself."

"When you're ready, Wynter, play the CD. Allow your heartache to heal. If not today, then when?"

If not today, then when? That line hit me like a strike of lightning.

14

Goodbye

Today's the day. Lucas' ashes are now stored in a ceramic vase, handmade by his grandmother in South Africa. Although they didn't have a close relationship due to the distance, she's in Sydney to pay her respects and support Lucas' family during this tough time.

Lucas' parents have organised a small gathering at their home to commemorate his death. They've invited me to say something. I guess you could call it a eulogy. I've struggled to put the memory of Lucas into words. It's been haunting me over the last week. Trying not to stumble has been a challenge.

Mum and Ara stand besides me as we walk up Lucas' childhood home's patio. To think we grew up living only a few streets away from each other all these years, we could have been friends even before we reached high school. I wonder what that would have been like. Little us.

Mum rings the doorbell, and we're welcomed by Mr and Mrs Mensah, Lucas' parents. Cora is leaning against Junior's arm, the internal pain is taking all her energy to stay upright. Placing myself in her shoes, I'd be far from indestructible. Instead, I'd be the first to break and crumble.

"Thank you for being here today," Cora says calmly, placing her hand on mine. "It means a lot to us that you're here, Wynter. Thank you for being the friend Lucas needed."

They usher us into their living room, located past the kitchen area. The sunshine's rays stream through the sheer curtains, adding some brightness to the room. It warms us all, despite it being a much cooler autumn's day.

Scanning the room, there are only a handful of faces I recognise. Besides Lucas' family, there's Mrs Yieldeman, Mr Lee, and to my surprise, Stacey. She's sitting down on one of the three-seater lounges, wedged between two people. From their appearances alone, I assume they're her parents. It's quite eerie how much she resembles the man sitting to her right. The woman, on the other hand, has the same bright orange hair as hers.

Stacey spots me and motions her way over, with the man and woman following behind.

"Hi, Stacey, I didn't realise you'd be here."

"You must be Wynter." The lady steps in between me and Stacey and reaches out for an embrace. Her grip is strong, reminding me of Mum's. It makes me curious as to whether every mother's hug feels tight and secure, even when their little babies become full-grown teenagers.

"Yep, that's me," I confess.

When the lady lets go, she admires me for a good minute or two.

Stacey interrupts the silence, "Sorry about that, Wynter. My mum's love language is touch. She's a hugger." This explains why Stacey's one too. Makes sense.

"Nice to meet you, Mrs Jones. This is my mum, Faye, and my sister, Ara."

"So lovely to meet the family. Lucas always described you as his second Mum," she says, holding a comforting gaze towards Mum. Mum looks like a young child again, free of any pain, taking in the information as heartwarming news.

A floodgate of questions rushes through my already unclear mind. *How* does Stacey's family know Lucas? *Why* didn't Lucas tell me? *Why* didn't Stacey tell me? *Who* are they?

Mrs Mensah chimes in, interrupting my wandering thoughts.

"Please, help yourselves to some light refreshments, and there's some tea or coffee in the kitchen."

"Thank you, Mrs Mensah."

"And Wynter, dear, will you be ready to say a few words shortly? We're just waiting on a few more people."

"Of course," I reply. "As ready as I can be."

Is anyone ever ready to say a tribute in dedication to their best friend? Never would I have imagined being in this position, yet here I am.

"Wynter ..." Stacey speaks softly, close to a whisper. "We were supposed to tell you earlier, but then, all of this happened."

"We? As in you and Lucas? How do you know each other?"

"Long story cut short, Lucas was actually both excited and nervous for us to meet. He said he mentioned it briefly to you, and how we'd get along just fine."

Light bulb moment. It hits me that Stacey is the person Lucas was referring to during our walk.

"Do you have a history? Lucas never told me he had a girlfriend."

Stacey shivers and laughs, shrieking at that thought.

"Oh please, no. Lucas is my cousin. Cora and Dad are siblings. You wouldn't think we'd be related just by looking at us though, right?"

"Never even crossed my mind."

"Lucas' family spent two years living with us in California, back when he was just around seven years old. Because I have no siblings, I spent most of that time playing with Lucas and Guy. We'd spend hours on end outside, playing in the mud, riding our bikes, and kicking a ball. Poor Lucas could barely keep up. But never in a million years would Lucas join me in reading a book. 'Boring' is what he'd refer to it as."

"Look at him now ... I mean, well, how he was. With reading. Sorry, I can barely talk properly right now, I'm getting tongue-twisted. My nerves are getting the better of me."

"Wynter, he told us about the time he joined you for lunch, reading *We Were Liars*. I still can't believe he had the exact book in his bag. I didn't believe him at first, because, Lucas reading? Those two words would never have been together side-by-side in a sentence. But then I discovered your little book club."

"It was a good coincidence, in hindsight."

"It was. You know, Lucas struggled to make friends as a kid. He had a stutter, so most kids would make fun of him. He hated reading because one time a teacher made him read aloud to the class, and his stutter intensified. But maybe, he did love to read after all. He just needed someone special to read with ... without any judgement."

"I had no idea. He talks so much now. Before. He talked a lot."

"He grew out of it. I noticed over time, whenever his family would video call us, his stutter lessened."

Finding out about Lucas' past which I had zero knowledge about doesn't upset me. Instead, it makes me realise how strong of a person he is, looking past the bullies from such a young age and overcoming his stutter.

"Why didn't you mention you were his cousin when we first met?"

"To be honest, I don't know. Lucas was the one who always made proper introductions. He said he was waiting for you to figure it out, as though we were characters in a mystery novel. I told him that would be the most trivial mystery of all time." A thought of Lucas sneaks its way, lifting the corners of my lips as I remember his often bizarre but wonderful ideas.

Stacey adds, "And at the same time, I didn't want to be like, 'Hey, I'm Lucas' cousin' as though that would give me extra brownie points towards an instant friendship with you."

"Do you miss him?"

Stacey holds her breath a few seconds longer than normal before releasing a soft but heavy sigh. Her eyebrows narrow and eyes jitter.

"I wish we could have spent more time together. We spent more time apart than we did together, even if I were to add up all those days they lived with us."

A single tear escapes from Stacey's eye, but she quickly wipes it dry.

Mrs Mensah clears her throat. "Thank you all for coming. Our family is grateful for the loving support we've received. Today, as we remember the life Lucas lived, we wanted to invite his best friend, Wynter, to share a few words. Wynter was the light of Lucas' days. He found a reason to be grateful daily because of her. We're forever thankful for you, Wynter."

There are already tears floating around the room. Mr Mensah assists me to join them, and there's a long pause of silence while I take in a deep breath before reading his eulogy. Mum gives me a reassuring smile and reminders of daily affirmations travel from her heart to mine.

"Thank you Mr and Mrs Mensah and Guy. Honestly, I almost didn't think I could do this today. There hasn't been a single day where I haven't cried myself to sleep, wishing to see Lucas just one more time. But the reality is, that won't happen in this lifetime.

"Every thought consuming my mind is centred around him. Time is cruel, yet the time we spent together, I'll forever cherish. Lucas reminded me how beautiful life is. When things were far from rainbows and butterflies, he still shared a positive reasoning. He always, always gave me a reason to smile. Even in the rain.

"It's been a burden knowing he died on his way to give me something. Day in and day out, I felt angry at him for putting his life at risk for something that could have waited until the following morning. But it just goes to show how much of a loving person he is. He didn't want to wait to share a beautiful gift. He wanted the person receiving it to be smiling then and there. Not the next hour, not the next day.

"This CD right here, I couldn't bring myself to play. I didn't want to find out what it held. Miss Xi, thank you for helping me to see through a less clouded pair of eyes because what this CD holds is Lucas. A part of him that represents just how much of a kind-spirited person he was. How much he valued friendship.

"So, to remember Lucas today, I want to share this with you all. Because I can probably speak for all of us, that he's touched our hearts in more ways than one. And, he never quite got the chance to be a solo performer, so here's his first piece, titled *Dear Wynter*."

I play the CD, ensuring the volume is set high enough for everyone to hear. Mr and Mrs Mensah are holding hands tightly and Guy has his arm wrapped around his mum's shoulder. Everyone holds their breath as the CD starts to play Lucas' graceful voice that sings in perfect harmony to the keys he plays on the piano.

Dear Wynter,
You're the words floating on this page,
You're every note forming this tune.
I think back to the day you're sitting alone,
With just a book to keep you safe.
Little did I know,
You'd be my safeguard too.

Dear Wynter,
You're the thoughts written on this page,
You're every light reflecting on my mind.
I think back to the day raindrops are landing on you,
With just my warmth to keep you safe.
Little did I know,
You'd be my shelter too.

Dear Wynter,
You're the beat to my heart,
You're every step marked with a smile.
I think back to the days I'm side by side with you.

Our worlds collided into one.
Little did we know,
We'd be best friends too.

Dear Wynter,
This is only our beginning,
I promise to you.

The song ends and Miss Xi is right, there's not a dry eye in the room.
Guy is choking up, realising that his brother finished the piece after all.
An onset of tears scatters across my face and blurs my 20/20 vision.
It's only goodbye, for now, Lucas. I promise.

15

Second Goodbye

MY KEYBOARD IS NO longer hidden behind closed doors. Lucas would have wanted me to continue playing music. He had more confidence in my ability than I ever did. He would often say he knew talent when he saw one. No matter how often I failed to sing in tune, or if it took me several pauses to read the notes before playing them, Lucas was patient and encouraging.

"Trust me, it just takes practise. Anyone can sing, as long as they're willing to," he'd say.

As I sit with my hands above the keys, I close my eyes and allow my fingers to drift into a melody. The entire song, I sing from the core of my heart.

Dear Lucas,
You're the words buried in my heart,
You're every underrated perfect piece of art.
A wave of emotions, captivating and real,
Without a mask to hide behind.
You radiate the warmest smile,
Even when you're feeling down.

Dear Lucas,
You're the memory buried in my mind,
You're every happy chapter in this story.
A rare gem, shining endlessly.
Always with a kind heart,
Rain, hail or shine.

Dear Lucas,
You inspire everyone you meet.
This is only a quick goodbye,
Until we meet again...

"Goodbye, Lucas, for now. I hope you liked the song."

16

Road Trip

It's Mum's idea. With the next two weeks off school, instead of being housebound, Mum planned a family road trip for the first week. She invited Lucas' family, but Cora isn't ready to go on a trip with one less son yet. It's understandable, and Mum respects her decision.

It's been a while since we've been on a family holiday. I can't quite remember what to pack and how much. Ara has a suitcase plus two bags filled with many different outfits, enough to cover any sort of weather we come across.

"Ara, we're not relocating. Are you sure you packed enough there?" Mum jokes.

"You can never be over-prepared, Mum. The weatherman is rarely right these days."

"I can't argue with you on that," Mum agrees.

Mum looks across the hall and peeps into my room. "I take it you haven't started packing yet?"

"I'm just, well, I don't know how to 'holiday' I guess."

"We leave at dawn to avoid traffic. It'll be a three-hour drive to Canberra. Once we get there we'll stop by Maccas for breakfast."

"That means I better get packing then. Will it be really cold?"

Mum lays my suitcase open on my bed and walks back and forth from my wardrobe to the suitcase, filling it with clothes.

"Your jacket, you can leave out. You'll be wearing it when we leave," she hints.

"Mum, can I bring my pillow?" Something about sleeping on hotel pillows irks me even though they're changed for each guest.

"As long as you're happy to carry it."

I nod and shake her hand. It's a done deal.

The last time we travelled to Canberra, I must have been around four years old. Ara begged Mum for weeks to go because all her friends had been to Questacon and she was missing out. After quite the debate, which Ara was an expert at even back then, Mum gave in. When we stepped foot into the large entryway, Ara's eyes enlarged with unmatched excitement. She spent hours upon hours exploring every section while Mum tugged me along.

This time, Ara desperately wants to visit Canberra to explore the museums. The only thing on my bucket list whilst there is to visit the National Library of Australia. In any city we visit, I make it a mission to go to the local library. It's incredible how rows and rows of books can have a therapeutic effect. Lucas and I would often go to libraries together during the school holidays. Not to study, but to get lost in the pages of the many hardbacks we read through.

***

Ara sits in the passenger seat—it's been 'hers' since she was old enough to sit there. There's something about being in charge of the songs that play while Mum drives that makes her feel happy and accomplished. I don't mind because I have the entire backseat to myself. But today, the backseats are filled with several bags because of the limited boot space for all of our luggage—well, mainly Ara's.

"What shall we listen to?" Ara chants, knowing quite well that she'll be answering her own question.

Before Mum manoeuvres out of the driveway, Pink's *Beam Me Up* starts playing.

"Anything else less depressing?" Mum asks.

Ara loves to belt love songs at the top of her lungs, but maybe this road trip isn't the best drive for that. I mean, we're trying to keep ourselves distracted from all the recent heartbreak.

Normally Ara would find a way to make her reasoning win, but I notice she looks in the sun visor mirror to observe the expression on my face. She mouths *I'm sorry* and rummages through the CD case to find a different album.

"It's okay, Ara, honestly. Belt your heart out."

I realise that changing the song won't change the fact that Lucas is gone. It doesn't matter what song plays, I'll constantly be reminded of him—music was ingrained in his blood. No matter what genre, Lucas had the unique talent to play it on the piano, even if it was the first time hearing the song.

The lyrics are drowned out by the inner workings of my brain. My eyes are sealed, and I'm reminded of the day Lucas and I would read the dedication page of a book, and he'd turn the words into lyrics, singing with his celebrity-worthy voice along with a piano. We'd try to match the beat to the meaning behind the sentence. Lucas recorded every thirty-second song because he wanted to piece them all together one day. Imagine that, a soundtrack of dedications. I wonder where he saved the recordings. It would be nice to hear his voice again.

There's a sudden halt.

My mind refocuses back to the present. Mum's breathing is heavy as she adjusts her posture.

"I'm so sorry!" she cries.

I peer out the window and notice she's one or two metres away from hitting a barbed wire fence.

Her hands cover her face as she weeps.

"I thought I could push aside my fears," Mum admits.

Ara consoles Mum and reaches across to hug her as best she can. "Mum, it's okay. We're all okay."

My mind has been consumed by thoughts of losing Lucas that I had forgotten about others suffering sadness too. Mum's may be different to mine, but incomparable as loss is loss. I get it. Lucas' death has broken her heart ten-fold; witnessing me crumble, and magnifying her longing to be with Dad again. To see us all together, a complete family. Lucas' accident has shifted her thoughts all the way back to the day I was born.

"Mum, I'm so sorry. I should have known."

Mum sobs, but she nods her head sideways. "There's nothing to be sorry about, sweetie. I should have been more open about my anxiety with driving again. I just didn't know how without bringing up Lucas' accident. It's already been a lot for you to handle."

"Mum ..." I pause, realising I need to choose my words carefully. "Dad's accident ... How did you get through it?" I ask, without knowing the finer details of the accident, other than Dad didn't survive it.

"I don't know if I'm through it. If I ever will. I get by. I've learned to continue living, especially with you and Ara giving me purpose. But it still hurts. I try to think of all the good times we shared together, but then I start to yearn for those times to be good times he could have had with his daughters, too."

"Time is so cruel," I murmur.

Although I was a newborn when Dad died, his accident haunts Mum to this day. Ara and I both sense it, but hearing Mum's words confirms it. Dad's accident. Tragic is an understatement.

"It was all unexpected and happened sooner than anyone can recall." Mum blows her nose before she carries on. "Your dad had left the hospital just a few hours after you were born to pick Ara up from Drew and Luna's. They kindly offered to babysit. In the same hour, Ye-jun's SUV, or what was left of it, was breaking news, live on air."

It crushes my heart to think how a sudden turn of events can happen in just one click. Without warning. An event no-one could have ever seen coming.

"You see, a careless driver, who had one too many drinks, performed an illegal U-turn on the highway. He crashed straight into your dad's car. The size of the damage, it's an image I'll never forget."

"How did you find out?"

"Besides hearing sirens blaring from all directions? I still remember the distressed look on the paramedic's face. She wanted to tell me personally after finding out I was in the same hospital he was rushed to. Even though they arrived at the scene within minutes, the impact was far too strong. I remember she was trying to stop herself from sobbing, and barely choked out the words, 'we tried all we could' to keep your dad's heart from failing, but he passed away within minutes."

That horrible news would have been the reason behind Mum's fear of driving. I can't blame her for that.

Mum's still in tears, her eyes are tender and screaming for better days.

Ara continues to comfort Mum. "We can turn back, Mum. Canberra can wait."

Thankfully we're only a mere ten minutes away from home, so Ara contacts Drew, who lives two houses away from ours, to drive us back.

Drew is in his thirties, married to the sweetest wife, Luna, and a dad to the cutest twin toddlers, Delilah and Rose. Drew's someone who the whole neighbourhood can depend on. He never makes anyone feel bad asking for help, or feel like they're a nuisance. Luna is the most supportive wife and often bakes the softest, gooiest choc-chip cookies for the entire street for no occasion, simply out of kindness.

After a short wait, Mum sees Drew to the rescue from her rearview mirror. He had caught the next bus that stopped closest to where we sat stranded.

Mum hops out of the driver's seat and falls into Drew's embrace, thanking him no less than a hundred times.

"Don't even worry 'bout it, yeah?" Drew says with his hands on Mum's shoulders, calming her down.

"Thanks, Drew," Ara and I say simultaneously.

"Any time. I got ya backs. Now let's get ya guys back home."

Normally, I sit behind the passenger's seat, but I make a conscious effort to sit in the middle so that I can hold Mum's hand the entire drive back home. Whilst her body is calmer, her hands are still shaking.

"You're okay, Mum. We've got you."

Ara decides to stop the music. The rest of the drive home is quiet, but we all soak it in, remembering how sometimes the silence can be deafening but it can also mend a broken heart.

When we reach home, Drew hands the keys over to Ara. His next instant reaction is to wave at Delilah and Rose who are playing on their front lawn, pulling out dandelions and blowing them in all directions, wherever the wind allows. Luna waves from afar with the same smile Mum gives to remind me that everything will be okay.

"Thanks again, Drew," Ara says. "Give the twins a hug from us."

"Call us anytime, don't ya worry 'bout the time. If it's two in the mornin' or ten at night. Always happy to help."

Drew runs back to his twins, chasing them and pretending to be a giant dinosaur. Delilah and Rose giggle, running in opposite ways. Ten little steps for them equates to one leap for Drew. He catches them quickly and squeezes them in for a big dinosaur hug. Luna watches in admiration before joining in.

Seeing this is a timely reminder that the world carries on, no matter what your day is like. That happiness still exists. Today can feel like a struggle, but tomorrow could be life-changing. You just never know what lies ahead.

Today though, Mum needs Ara and I. So we muster up any of our own hidden anxieties and force the knots in our stomachs to ease in order to be the stronghold Mum needs.

"I'm so sorry, this was supposed to be a fun family trip."

There's a disheartened tone in Mum's voice as she apologises. Not only has she just felt terrified behind the wheel, but the guilt is eating her up.

"Mum, Ara and I are exactly where we're supposed to be. Right here, right now. We love you, Mum."

17

Hang Out

THE LAST TIME I logged into Facebook, Lucas was still here. Scrolling through my newsfeed can be draining. It feels mindless almost, only to find 'happy' moments where everyone appears to be living the picture-perfect dream. From spectacular holiday destinations by the ocean, to five-star Michelin dishes captured perfectly in a photograph for viewing pleasure, to action shots from a much awaited concert or live show, and to the flawless family photoshoots where everyone is posed like a model, showing off their pearly whites. I wonder how much of it is real. No-one shows the unfiltered versions after all.

After checking my emails earlier in the day, it prompted me to check Facebook as there are several new messages from Stacey. She has my mobile number but it seems she prefers using social media to communicate. When it comes to being active online, Stacey's high up in the ladder and I struggle to climb the first step.

It takes me a moment to remember my password. Creativity isn't exactly my forte when it comes to security. *Sunflower123*—my favourite flower, which, in hindsight, isn't a clever idea. It would have been smarter to have my least favourite flower instead so it would be harder for others to guess, but then again, there's no such thing as that.

Every flower makes my heart glow. Sunflowers in particular because of their bright yellow petals and the fact that a young sunflower's face follows the sun from sunrise to sunset every day until maturity. In some ways, it's like a young child looking up to their parents, constantly being their shadow, but admiring them in awe like they're the sun providing them with light and joy. Then they reach maturity, and whilst they still depend on their parents, it's not a constant attachment.

There's the option to change my password, but the reality is, the probability of someone hacking into my account is extremely low. I'm sure their own lives will have more highlights in one day than I have in one year.

As I log in, my inbox is flooded with messages from Stacey.

Stacey: Hey Wynter, didn't get to say bye after the funeral today. Sorry, my parents have a tight schedule so we had to leave soon after the eulogy. I'm still crying from it. You guys had a beautiful friendship.

Stacey: Hey Wynter, are you doing anything on Friday? Do you want to hang out?

Stacey: Me again ... I lost your number. Actually, I lost my phone! My parents aren't replacing it until I pass all my classes. So I'm contacting you here instead.

Stacey: Sorry for bugging you. Just checking you're okay? I know the last week has been hard on you. I'm here if you need a friend.

Stacey: Okay, last message, I swear! If you're free Friday night, come over for dinner. Of course, Mrs Hope and Ara can come too if they'd like. Mum will be cooking Shepherd's Pie :)

Technically I *am* free on Friday night, which is already tonight, now that our Canberra trip is off the table. If only I had checked my messages earlier so I'd have more time to weigh out the pros and cons more specifically. I'm not sure I know how to *hang out* the way Stacey imagines. When we're at school, we have something in common. But take that one commonality away and it suddenly feels like building a friendship isn't second nature. When Lucas and I would hang out, we both had a love for music and books. It was more than enough for us. It kept our conversations going for hours on end. I just can't see the same thing happening with Stacey. She's a lot more daring and would be the first to put her hand up to go skydiving.

Lucas and I saw the world through a different pair of binoculars. We didn't need to do anything the world viewed as exciting or adventurous to enjoy each other's company. I could spend the entire afternoon captivated by the melodies he plays on the keyboard.

As I think about a reply, I notice that Stacey's online and has started typing another message. Before I start typing, I receive a new message from her.

Stacey: *Yay, you're finally online! Mum's prepping dinner now. Are you guys coming?*

The pressure of having to reply instantly suffocates me slowly. Quickly gathering my thoughts and translating them into words is a life skill I lack. How can people think on the spot with little to no notice? This is probably another reason why I'm barely online. I'm not an instant messaging type of person. Give me a pen and paper instead, and I'll write a four-page letter.

Wynter: *Hey Stacey, thanks for the invitation. Sorry for the late reply, I don't check Facebook often. Our Canberra trip didn't go ahead, so we don't have anything planned for tonight. I'll let Mum and Ara know.*

In less than thirty seconds, Stacey has already replied.

Stacey: *Awesome! Come over anytime, but dinner will be ready at around 6pm. Luckily we're only a five-minute drive away from yours.*
Wynter: *See you then!*

Most teenagers my age would have had several sleepovers or hang outs by now. But not me. Stranded at home is where I feel most comfortable. Every corner feels inviting even after dark. Far from a designer display home, it's the cosy character it holds that I love the most. The ever growing changes, stamping marks of years gone by. The chiselled handrail by the staircase. How you need to nudge the bathroom door that tad bit extra to be able to free yourself. Or how it takes a good minute before the kitchen tap water starts to heat up. Even how one of our La-Z-Boys squeaks if it's reclined all the way. But it feels like home. A real home. All of it.

Even with Lucas, the funeral service was my first time inside his home. He would normally come over to ours because it felt like his second home since Mum and Ara were around often. There was always company.

Lucas' parents worked a lot, so after school, he'd come home to an empty house; well, what felt like one anyway since Guy spent the rest of the evening gaming on his computer. His parents owned a bakery several suburbs away, so they had early starts and late finishes. Their bakery is known for having the best tea bread and sugar bread in town. The whiff you get as you walk past is nothing short of heavenly. Lucas says it's his grandma's recipe from back home and it reminds Junior of his childhood.

Whenever Lucas was over, he'd either be playing on our piano downstairs, or reading a book with me in the lounge room. He loved that we all sat around the kitchen bench snacking on hot chips and gravy as we shared stories from our day. I loved sharing chips with him because he hated the crunchy ones whereas I couldn't stand the soggy ones. Thankfully we both liked having the same amount of chicken salt, so it worked out. Our tummies were always full.

"Might as well eat a packet of potato chips instead," Lucas says.
"You might as well have mashed potatoes."
"Let's call it even then. But seriously, these soggy chips are so good."
"I need some sort of crunch to them."
"I wonder how the chips feel about us having favourites."
"They have no feelings."
Lucas holds a chip up and changes his tone. "Ouch, that hurts, Wynter. We have feelings."
Lucas always finds a way to make me laugh. He never fails.

I make my way downstairs where I find Mum baking some banana bread. Whilst she's not the world's greatest cook, she sure can bake. The air smells inviting.

"Mmm smells delicious."

"Oh, thank you. I made a little extra because we had so many overripe bananas."

"That's not a bad thing. More to go around."

Mum pops the tray on the bench to allow it to cool down.

"Mum, Stacey's family invited us over for dinner tonight."

"That's kind of them! They were all so lovely when we met. Well, it's a good thing I made extra bread and haven't prepared dinner yet."

"And a good thing they're only a five minute drive …" I suddenly realise, just as the word escapes from my mouth, that we need to *drive* to theirs. How could it slip my mind so easily that we don't exactly have a driver right now. Ara's still an L-plater, so legally, she could drive us there with Mum in the passenger's seat, but that would only heighten Mum's anxiety. Ara isn't a bad driver, but Mum says she'd prefer a driving instructor to teach her, as they're used to being the passenger already. They can probably keep their nerves grounded more too.

"We can walk there." Ara joins the conversation. "A bit of fresh air will do us some good."

Mum redirects her attention to me, noticing I've gone quiet. "Is there anything on your mind, sweetheart?"

"No, nothing. It's okay."

The truth is, my anxiety is skyrocketing knowing hanging out with Stacey after school hours is outside my comfort zone. That I'm cheating on my best friend. I know Stacey has good intentions but building a friendship with her outside of school feels like it's the start of replacing Lucas. I never want that to happen.

"Wynter?" Mum says this knowing full well that there is definitely something eating me up inside.

"I just ... I don't think I'm ready for a new friendship."

"Oh, Wynter. Come over here." Mum pulls me in for a hug and strokes my hair as she does. "You'll be alright, sweetheart. Stacey is a wonderful friend. Being friends with her doesn't mean you're replacing Lucas, okay?"

"Okay ... It's just that, well, I don't know. Should I be happy so soon?"

"Lucas would have wanted you to be happy, yesterday."

Mum's right. Lucas would have been on my back about looking at the brighter side of things, anytime he sensed a cloud hovering over me.

"What's bugging you, Wynter?" Lucas asks.

"I'd like to say 'nothing' but my face says otherwise, I take it?"

"Not gonna lie, you're not the best at hiding how you're feeling."

"Do you think there's such a thing as being ugly and pretty?"

"As in how a person looks?"

"Yeah, I guess."

"We all find different things pretty and ugly. I mean, we don't all see things the same way."

"Do you think, maybe ... Well, never mind."

"No, I don't, Wynter."

"No you don't, what?"

"No, I don't think you're ugly. Is this what's bothering you? If anyone's called you that, remember it's their self-doubt, not yours."

I lean my head on Lucas' shoulder, hiding the tears that I fail to contain. "You're only saying that because you're my friend."

"Your honest friend."

"Thanks, Lucas."

"If it's any consolation, I look in the mirror and can't help but compare myself with Guy, the better-looking brother."

"You don't say," I joke.

"Wait ... Who called you ugly? Do you want me to—"

"It doesn't matter. I don't know them anyway. Just someone ... Well, no-one important."

Lucas lifts my downcast face by my chin. "Hey, listen, Wynter. You're not ugly. You're not even pretty. You're beautiful, okay? Inside and out. That's rare to find."

I bring my thoughts back to the present time. Mum's still embracing me and I can hear her heart beating gently as my head rests on her chest. She's calm, which is soothing.

I am braver than I think, stronger than I feel. I have the courage to face my fears.

18

Trust

THE DOORBELL CHIMES AS Mum presses it. Through the frosted glass, I can see a figure swiftly approaching the door.

"Hello! Come in, come in! So lovely to have you over."

As we enter their house, the first thought that comes to mind is, *wow*. Their walls are so high, the ceiling is beyond reach. The floors are made of marble, and there are gold ornaments on display. It feels like I just stepped into a palace.

Beyond the foyer, above the fireplace, sits a huge family portrait painted in oil paints.

"Take a seat, please. Make yourselves feel at home."

Mrs Jones reaches out for an intercom and dials it. "Stacey darlin', our guests are here. Hurry now."

For a moment, I thought maybe Stacey was on her way home, but no. From their grand staircase, Stacey glides down like she's floating on air.

"Wynter! Hey!" She's beyond excited to see me. "Come, let me show you around."

Stacey grabs me by the hand and the next thing I know, we're passing hallways with walls covered in family photos. They all look as though they've been professionally shot. The images are maga-zine-worthy.

"I was just in the middle of working on my music piece for school."

"Oh, what're you playing?"

"Come, I'll show you!"

We race upstairs, my feet trying to keep up with hers.

"Your home is incredible."

"It's only just starting to feel like home now. For a while, it felt as though I'd go crazy from the silence. You can hear even the softest footsteps approaching."

Stacey opens the French doors that lead into her bedroom.

"Wow, this is your room? It's as big as our whole house."

"My parents are a bit over the top with spoiling me because I'm an only child and they have this guilt of never being able to have a sibling for me. Not that that's an issue, but to them, it has been. They both come from big families, so you could imagine their disappointment in our small family of three. If they had the choice, they'd gladly have enough kids to form a soccer team."

"How's your music piece going?"

Attempting not to sound rude, I try to shift the conversation to a topic I'm more familiar with and comfortable talking about. Talking about having babies reminds me of how my parents struggled for so long before conceiving me.

Ara recalls being a toddler at the time, but even being so young, she sensed the stress and grief Mum felt after each miscarriage. Sometimes she spent hours on end in bed, during the middle of the day, while Ara played with Dad. Dad would be the one trying to keep it together, even though Ara knew Dad was also heartbroken. He gave Mum the time she needed to weep and for her body to heal and recover.

Stacey replies, "I just finished! Come listen."

Stacey isn't shy at all. Not only is she a future Olympian, but she's also most likely a Musician, too.

"I haven't had the chance to practise much, so it might need some fine-tuning. It's just an instrumental piece. I'm horrible at writing lyrics, unlike you and ... I'm sorry."

"It's okay. Lucas was a music genius."

Stacey unzips the case and takes out a glossy violin. Her movements are gentle now and her facial expression is in character. As she plays, my heart aches. The effect her composition has on my heartstrings, I wasn't expecting. Every note is perfect, but the feeling of the melody executes a calmness after the rain.

At the end of Stacey's performance, I clap, praising her talent.

"That was amazing, Stacey."

"Thank you, it sort of just escaped from me over the last couple of days. How's yours going?"

"It's on hold. I started when Lucas was still here. I'll need to look over it again."

"Well, we've still got a whole week off school. You'll get there."

Stacey moves and sits by her desk where her laptop is stationed. The screensaver is a photo of her with another girl at the beach who looks her age.

"Who's that?"

"That's Candice, my best friend in the U.S. That beach was our favourite spot. She was fond of collecting seashells and then making art out of them."

"Do you miss her?"

"Every day. Thankfully video calls exist. Plus, we're chatting online whenever we have a spare second anyway, so we stay up-to-date with each others' lives. Wanna see some photos?"

Stacey lets me sit by her desk and opens an album titled 'Besties.' But my eyes gravitate towards something else.

Stacey's Facebook messenger chat page is left open with the Besties folder floating above it. Below our recent chat, I see Candice's name, followed by Lucas'. I know it's wrong to invade someone else's privacy but I can't help but read the line of text that previews next to Lucas' name: *Good choice, she'll thank you for that, trust me.*

She? Besides Mrs Mensah, the only other 'she' in Lucas' life before Stacey arrived was me.

Stacey notices I'm not browsing through the album. She grabs the mouse and minimises the Facebook chat window.

"Sorry, I always forget to close other windows. Bad habit."

My mind is racing so fast that I'd probably outrace Stacey for once. *That's all that matters* replays in my mind, Mum's advice about trying my best. Right now, I'm trying my best to not intrude on Stacey's messages, but every nerve in my body is insisting that it's the missing piece to my incomplete puzzle. Context is everything and I just need reassurance that I'm overthinking all of this, that there's nothing to worry about.

"Lucas messaged you before he died?" I ask bluntly.

"Uh ... It's not important."

"Did he message you before he died? Were you the last person he spoke to? I need to know."

Stacey's quiet.

Without thinking clearly, I maximise the window again and click on the chat between her and Lucas so that the entire conversation is in full view.

Lucas: Woohoo, I've finally finished my music piece. I'm dedicating it to Wynter. It's called Dear Wynter.

Stacey: Aw, cute!

Lucas: I saved it on a CD. I want her to have the original copy and be the first to hear it before the class does.

Stacey: Then what are you waiting for?

Lucas: What do you mean?

Stacey: Why don't you give it to her now?

Lucas: Because it's 10pm and she sleeps early. I'll give it to her first thing tomorrow morning.

Stacey: Trust me, she'll appreciate the gesture if you gave it now. It'll be a sweet memory.

Lucas: Trust me, she'll appreciate me not interrupting her sleep.

Stacey: Stop being so lazy, Lucas. Just go.

Lucas: Fine ... You better be right about this. If Mrs Hope shuts the front door on me ...

Stacey: She doesn't have a single bad bone in her body. She'll probably ask you to stay for some tea or something.

Lucas: Okay, well I better go now then, before the night turns into day. See you tomorrow.

Stacey: Good choice, she'll thank you for that, trust me.

All this time I felt angry at myself for being the reason Lucas went out of his way to risk his life. To find out that his intention was otherwise crushes my soul.

"Please tell me this isn't true." I choke on my words and struggle to speak clearly.

Stacey's head is downcast. "Wynter, it's not what you think."

An onset of tears blur my ability to see but it's clear that Stacey's silhouette starts pacing back and forth in distress.

"I can't believe I actually thought we were friends. You kept this from me this whole time. This *whole time* I felt responsible for Lucas being out that night."

Stacey leans forward, attempting to hold my hand but I pull it away swiftly and take a step back, widening the distance between us.

"Wynter, I *wanted* to tell you. I just ... With our friendship growing, I don't know. I didn't know how."

"There's nothing real about this friendship. All you've proven tonight is that I barely even know you. I don't know you at all."

Stacey starts to sob, defeat plastered all across her face. This isn't the appearance of the strong Stacey I thought I knew.

"I didn't mean to, Wynter. I swear. If I knew how the night would end ... I didn't know ..."

"You ... You *made* him go ..."

"All I wanted was for Lucas to do something romantic for you. To show you how much he cared about you."

Suddenly my cheeks feel as though they're on fire and my head starts to ache.

"A romantic gesture? If you knew Lucas at all, you would have known our friendship didn't need any grand Hollywood-style gestures. We were *best friends*. He knew me well enough to know to wait until the morning. But I know now that he felt pressure to go so late … from you."

"I'm sorry, Wynter. I thought there was more to your friendship." Stacey breaks down crying, her hands wipe away at her eyes but the tears don't stop.

"Is it so hard to believe that two people can be best friends *without* falling in love? We're not living in some fairytale. Our friendship was perfect the way it was. You didn't need to try and inflict your own twist to it. Now nothing's ever going to be the same again."

"I'm sorry."

My blood is boiling. Stacey's presence is no longer calming, it rings anger to my ears. I run downstairs where Mum and Ara are helping Mrs Jones set up the dinner table.

I'm shaking as I stand before them. Mum lets go of the cutlery and runs over to me.

"We need to leave now, Mum."

"But sweetie, Mrs Jones has just—"

"*Now*, Mum. I'm leaving. With or without you."

I run for the front exit and make my way back home under the moonlit sky. I don't turn around, not once, to see if Mum and Ara are following.

For the first time in my entire existence, I scream at the top of my lungs without caring about strangers in the neighbourhood seeing me this way.

Lucas should still be here.

19
You and Me Both

I LAY IN BED under the doona, which traps the warm air. It's a struggle to breathe freely, but it's not as painful as the hurt circulating in my body. Pepper makes himself cosy, comfortably nested at the end of my bed.

I think back to a time when each day was easy-going. When my biggest problem was failing Maths.

"What's your favourite word?" Lucas asks before taking a bite of his burger.

"Mmm ... Aloha. It can mean both hello and goodbye. Something is moving about that."

"Mine's racecar," Lucas says proudly.

"Racecar?"

"Because it's spelled the same way forwards and backwards. I've always found palindromes interesting. Did you know that even some sentences can be palindromes? I came across a cool one the other day: A nut for a jar of tuna."

It takes me a moment to mentally picture spelling it backwards.

"That's pretty cool. What's your least favourite word?"

Lucas takes a moment to meditate on the question.

"Regret."

"That's a good one. I'm not sure what mine is."

"When you know it, you'll know it."

"Sometimes I regret not saying enough, especially to defend myself from Ali."

"No-one's perfect. At least you haven't stooped down to her level. Most people in your shoes would act all vengeful and lose sight of what really matters."

"Do you think you and I will still be friends after we've graduated?"

"Who, us? That's not even a question. We still have to travel around the globe and stop by every bookshop," Lucas replies.

"Only after we've spent the years beforehand working in one, we need funds for a big trip like that."

"Well lucky for us we're known by every local bookshop around. They'll hire us in a heartbeat."

"And then I'll be distracted by all the books."

"You and me both," Lucas says smiling. "You and me both."

You and me both. That's how life was supposed to be like. Now it's just me and the memory of you, Lucas. Just when I thought I was on the path to moving forward, I've taken ten steps back.

Mum and Ara attempt to console me, but my lifelessness under the covers gives them the indication to give me some space.

Our one-way ticket to the world will never happen because exploring every bookshop without Lucas doesn't have the same excitement anymore. While he sleeps peacefully, I struggle to close my eyes and keep them shut without any strain.

Pepper positions his head on my leg. Maybe he can sense my pain, just like how Ara as a toddler could sense Mum's.

"Did you know Lucas always wanted to travel the world?"

Pepper doesn't react, he continues to rest on my leg, eyes drifting off into sleep.

"We were supposed to have a one-way ticket to the world. Travelling from bookshop to bookshop and from library to library."

Again, Pepper doesn't budge.

"Lucas, why did you listen to Stacey?"

I bury my face into my pillow and my tears soak through, revealing the agony my whole being holds.

How can Stacey wake up each morning and go about her day as though she wasn't the reason why Lucas left his home that evening? How has she been able to go to school every day, focus on all her work, plus attend his funeral, without a single trace of guilt? How?

I stroke Pepper's soft fur, it's just about the only form of comfort amidst the heartache.

Right now, my judgement is clouded but does that mean I'm not conscious? Lucas would have prompted me to use my five senses in this very moment in an attempt to ignite some joy. If he had a show of medals for the number of times he successfully spun a negative into a positive, he'd be on a wall of fame. And what have I learned from being his trainee in the world of 'using your five senses'? That I'm no superhero like Lucas. I can't move past resentment. I can't spin my senses into a promising thought. All I can think about is how Stacey hid a truth that could have helped with the healing process of losing my best friend.

I see disappointment.

I hear disappointment.

I taste disappointment.

I smell disappointment.

And I feel disappointment.

Disappointment has always hit me harder than any other emotion. You have this expectation of what you or someone else is capable of, of how you perceive someone, and all the trust can be broken by one action that leads to disappointment. At first, I felt rage towards Stacey, but now disappointment has knocked on the door, inviting itself in.

Lucas would have pointed me in the right direction to help me move past these thoughts. Although I realise I'm the only one who can help me. I need to find a way before I spiral into a vortex of madness.

I unravel from the safety of my doona and change out of my pyjamas into track pants and a windproof jacket.

Mum and Ara stare at me confused as I enter the kitchen, as though they're now wandering in the same dream as each other's.

"Wynter, sweetheart, are you okay?" Mum asks, although, by the shocked look on both their faces, I could ask the same question in return.

"Let's go," I instruct them. "While we still have time."

20

Off-Track

WHY DO THE SAYINGS 'get lost in a book' and 'get lost in nature' exist? Those words have always intrigued Lucas and I. Getting lost in a book, we experienced first-hand without any warning. As you turn the pages of a novel, you somehow get pulled in and the words become an extension of your imagination, and suddenly the two worlds collide—reality and fiction.

The first time Ara let me borrow her book, *A Walk To Remember*, I finally understood the hype of 'getting lost in a book' because all it takes is finding that one book that sparks your interest and the next thing you know, you're a certified bookworm.

Ever since then, my motto has been: *Never judge a book by its movie.* Because the truth is, the book is usually always superior. In *A Walk To Remember*, the text made it so clear as to why Sparks' titled the book exactly that, whereas the movie had you second-guessing.

One far-from-ideal winter's day, Lucas and I decided to test the same theory about nature.

"Let's start with an easy hike," I say whilst flipping through the pages of a Blue Mountains Bushwalking book.

"Let's try a more challenging one, otherwise, can we really get lost in nature? Literally and figuratively speaking, that is."

"Let's go straight to a hard graded one, then?"

"Okay. A hard one it is."

"Are you sure you're ready for this? I mean, the most sports we do is walking Pepper around the neighbourhood."

"Hiking is practically walking, right? Just with a different surrounding."

With eyes sealed tightly, I skim my finger down the page where all the hikes are listed. "Where will our grand hiking adventure be?"

And then my finger stops.

"Glenbrook Creek," I announce.

"Our first off-track adventure along Glenbrook Creek."

"Off-track makes it sound harder than I anticipated," I say, regretting what I've selected.

"Come on, let's get ready. There's no turning back now."

Lucas and I barely survived that day. It took us triple the time it takes experienced hikers to complete the same trail. Let's just say we literally got lost in nature. We didn't have time to stop and smell the roses, or bottlebrush trees in that regard, because we were in a race against time to make it to the end of the track before the sun set. We completely underestimated how long it would take us, especially with our hiking capability or lack thereof. Never again, we told ourselves.

Yet here I am today, facing the same track Lucas and I got through together, only this time I have Mum and Ara to get lost with. As we hop off the train, Ara checks the map she quickly printed out before leaving home hurriedly, ensuring we find the starting point without already getting lost.

Ara is the fittest and most ready to go. Mum is apprehensive but agrees to take part, relaying that it'll be a good chance for all of us to escape the suburban life for a day and truly appreciate time in nature.

"It sure is cold today," Ara announces the obvious.

"You'll feel warmer as soon as we get moving. It'll take a few hours to complete this track. And that's provided we stay on track," I say.

"Let's get going then," Ara leads the way with her natural leadership skills.

I trail behind to immerse myself in the clean air. The smell is refreshing, nostalgic almost, and bids me to stamp this moment in my memory bank.

To think that every step I'm taking, Lucas has walked in. Within the deep ground that sits below my worn-out shoes are Lucas' footprints, precise and with purpose. Every step he took had meaning. It meant pushing through despite being the least athletic person to walk the track. It meant continuing even when his brain was urging him to quit.

We kept each other alive that day, again, literally and figuratively. The mental boost we needed to persevere, we found in each other.

Ara is at least twenty metres ahead of Mum and I, navigating her way through the overgrown grass, forming a clearer pathway for us as she does.

"COOEE!" Ara shouts.

My heart skips a beat and my brain winds back time again to my bushwalk with Lucas. Just one word. That's all it took to send signals to my brain followed by a pinch to the heart, reminding me of Lucas' voice.

"We need a code word in case we get separated somehow," I say, nervous at the thought of hiking through overgrown bushland.

"Cooee," Lucas replies instantly, as though he's given this some deep thought already.

"Cooee?"

"Here, listen. You need to shout it out like this, COO-EE! And then it'll echo loud enough to travel far and wide, and once I hear it, I'll shout it back so that you know I've heard your call for help." There's a shrill rising emphasis on the 'ee' part.

"I'm not sure I can shout that loudly."

"Oh, you will if you need help. Did you know the word originated with the Aboriginals? From the Dharug language actually, which is a pretty neat coincidence because Glenbrook is on Dharug land."

"You love your history, don't you?"

"Everything has a history. That's the beauty of it."

"Cooee ..."

"You'll need to practise shouting louder than that. COO-EE! It translates to 'come here'."

"So if I'm lost, and I shout out cooee, it means you'll navigate your way to the sound of my voice? And when you say it back, I'll make my way towards yours? So we're basically saying 'come here' to each other at the same time. Huh."

"COO-EE!" Lucas yells and then reaches over to hold my hand.

"Pretty sure you used it in the wrong context. It's not a replacement word for 'come here'," I say as he pulls me along by the hand.

"Just come here already. Let's stay close to each other so we won't have to use that word in the correct context, how does that sound?"

"That's more reassuring. If I literally get lost in nature, trust me, I won't survive the night."

"Well then, cooee, let's get lost figuratively."

And that's exactly what happens. With several detours along the way.

Ara finally decides to take a pit stop by the creek to admire its glimmering charm. She's barely puffing, whereas Mum and I are drastically in need of water.

"Don't drink too much yet," Ara says. "Or you'll run out of water before we're even halfway to the finish line."

"But ..." Mum says, trying to catch her breath.

"Come here," Ara directs. "Just stare at the creek for a while, it's quite mesmerising. You'll forget you're tired."

Mum and I lean on each other for support and then sit on the sandy ground by the edge of the creek. The sun shines on the water, making it sparkle so sublimely.

Ara's right. Just like that I'm transported to a place of calm. A worry-free mindset. A place without any hurt or pain or anger or agony or sadness or regret.

Just pure serenity.

Mum looks into the distance. "It's been a long time since I've felt this calm. I guess all I had to do was travel a little farther away from the comfort of home."

"I wish we could take this feeling home with us. It's exhausting feeling every emotion under the sun all at once."

"You've been so strong, Wynter. Remember, you're only sixteen. You're not supposed to have it all together one hundred percent of the time. No-one is. We're all imperfect, but the important thing is, we never stop trying. To be kind. To be forgiving. To be honest. And we never stop trying to face our fears."

Mum takes a deep breath before she continues.

"After your dad died, I thought I could never drive again. For a while, I couldn't even sit in a car, especially with you as a baby and Ara as a toddler. My fear ate all the joy inside me I once had. It was a struggle to find myself again, even to just smile. But I needed to be a mother that both you and Ara could depend on. So slowly, I started facing my fear. At the start, I only reversed the car to the end of our driveway and that's as far as I got. But it was still a step. Turning the ignition on triggered so many horrible memories from the day your dad died but I needed to let myself remember them, to get over them."

"I keep getting flashbacks of Lucas."

"And that's okay, sweetheart. Hold onto them, they're not a bad thing."

"It makes me miss him being around. So many things remind me of him, Mum."

"You'll never stop missing him, just like how I miss your dad every single day. But, you'll have to learn to live life without him."

Mum places her palm on top of my hand. We sit together for another five minutes before we have to keep trekking to stay on track with the time ticking away.

How do you learn to live without someone who has been a huge part of your life? I hurry my pace to catch up to Ara, who is still full of energy, without any sign of tiredness.

"Do you remember how you wanted me to read *We Were Liars* so badly before?" I ask her.

"Yes, of course. I was so glad you loved it."

"Did I ever tell you that book brought me and Lucas together?"

"No, what do you mean?"

"Well, I was sitting alone at school during lunch—"

"Wynter! I told you to come and sit with me if you had no-one to sit with yet, remember?"

"I know … It's just … I was nervous and anxious. I just wanted to escape the noise. Everyone already had their own friendship circles happening. I didn't know how to step in …"

"Ah! I feel horrible now. I would have been there for you, Wynter. You know that, right?"

"I know … I'm sorry. I know to go to you for anything and everything. I just … I just didn't want to embarrass you. You know, hanging out with your little sister at school."

"Nothing is embarrassing about being nice to someone, especially if they're family."

"You're right …"

"Well, just remember for next time, I'm here, yeah? What were you saying about *We Were Liars* bringing you and Lucas together? Sorry, I cut your story short."

"I was about to read it, I had it out already. And then this shadow hovers over me. It was Lucas'. He looked familiar at the time, I just couldn't figure out how until he explained to me that he once went to each house in our neighbourhood to sell chocolate bars, and I was the only person who bought one from him. It was to raise funds for his Year 6 Farewell. If I knew, I would have asked Mum to buy the whole box."

"So you technically already met before high school then?"

"Technically, yes. He was so kind, even back then. He didn't end the day with sadness written on his face even though after hours of walking from house to house, he only made one dollar."

"Lucas has always been likeable," Ara reminisces.

"He has, and that lunchtime when all I had was a book in hand, he asked to sit with me. He had the same book in his bag. I couldn't believe it. What are the chances, right? Who would have known that book could bring us together."

"Well, I'm glad I kept pestering you to read it then. It all worked out." Ara's smiling, reflecting on the chain of events that lead to an unbreakable friendship.

"I just ... I just didn't realise that building a close friendship would mean it would shatter my heart if it were to end."

"No-one thinks of losing loved ones. It happens, but we can't control when that time comes."

Time is borrowed, for everyone. When the final seconds start ticking, we could have no idea until it strikes. I hope Lucas' final seconds were free from pain.

Mum catches up to me and Ara, hugging us both from the back.

"You two ... are the *absolute* light to my world."

"Love you, Mum," Ara and I say in sync.

We follow Lucas' buried footsteps to the end of the track, where we admire the warm hues of pinks and oranges and yellows and reds as the brightest star in the sky begins to set.

21

Square One

M R LENNARD HANDS OUT small cards to each of us, revealing a number from one through to sixteen. To my disappointment, mine is number two. This means I'll be the second student to perform my musical piece.

Whilst performing may come easy to some, there's a reason why I only write music in the safety net of my bedroom walls. There's no judgement there and I can execute my compositions as vulnerable as I need them to be.

Dylan King is the first to perform and he's far from nervous. He's known by the whole school to be the next newly found talent if Australian Idol were to ever be back on television. Dylan's been singing since he was seven years old and his voice is unmistakable.

There was a period where his voice was more high-pitched as he went through puberty, but his voice breaking randomly was out of his control. Once his vocal cords developed, he was able to make it sound angelic again. He's been going to singing lessons for so many years and performing at end-of-year concerts, which makes going first in class today a breeze for him, but increases anxiety for everyone else.

The bar is set high.

Not that it's a competition, it just makes the whole event intimidating. Mr Lennard marks us all individually without comparison. Well, besides the checklist he needs to follow as part of the assessment requirement. The last time I had to play the piano in front of the class, I froze. Literally. My body felt paralysed. After several attempts, it started feeding into our class time so Mr Lennard had no other choice but to grade my presentation with an F.

As defeating as that was, Mum was there to remind me that not all performers are comfortable in the spotlight. She was proud of me for being able to *try* by setting everything up in front of an audience and walking up on stage. Even though I froze, she looked past that and acknowledged my bravery for being in the limelight knowing that it makes my stomach churn.

Today feels different though. I feel nervous but ready. Lucas inspired the words and musical notes I'll soon be playing.

But back to Dylan, first. He adjusts the stand and tests the microphone to ensure the volume is set correctly and there's no feedback coming from the speakers. When Mr Lennard motions a thumbs up, the music track starts to play and Dylan closes his eyes, ready to sing the first line in perfect harmony.

I'm surprised by his song choice, *Love Me Like You Do* by Ellie Goulding, but Dylan somehow manages to make the song sound flawless. The rhythm is a slower pace, revealing the wonder in his voice. It slips my mind that I'm up next because Dylan's performance is so captivating. No-one looks away. We're all entrapped by his heartwarming piece.

Dylan sings the final line so effortlessly, sending chills down our spines. Even though I've heard the song many times before, it sounded like I was listening to it for the first time. He has a way with words through songs.

This is it. It's my turn. My pulse pumps a million beats per minute and it feels as though I'm on a one-way ticket to a heart attack.

"Wynter, are you ready?" Mr Lennard asks, allowing me to turn back if I can't fight the stage fright. He walks towards me so that my peers aren't able to hear what he says next. "Your best is all I can ask for. Lucas would have been proud, no matter the outcome."

I wasn't expecting to hear Lucas' name at this moment from someone else. It forces my mind to remember why I wrote this piece in the first place.

"Square One," I say, trembling as I speak into the microphone and adjust my sitting position by the piano.

I clear my throat. "This is a song Lucas, my best friend, inspired me to write. He reminded me that sometimes all you have to do is go back to square one and maybe that's where inspiration can stem from."

My fingers play the intro chords before my voice follows suit. It doesn't matter that I'm tone-deaf with my singing, I know in my heart that this musical piece needs to be accompanied by these lyrics ...

Everyone says you had the kindest smile,
I didn't get to see.
Everyone says you had the warmest hug,
I didn't get to feel.
Everyone says you had a comforting scent,
I didn't get to smell.
Everyone says you had the best treats,
I didn't get to taste.

Everyone says you had the friendliest voice,
I didn't get to hear.

If the clock turned back an hour,
Would it mean you'd still be here?
Would you then feel real?

Everyone says you had the best works of art,
I didn't get to see.
Everyone says you had the softest hand,
I didn't get to feel.
Everyone says you had a woody cologne,
I didn't get to smell.
Everyone says you had delicious dishes,
I didn't get to taste.
Everyone says you had a charming voice,
I didn't get to hear.

If the clock turned back an hour,
Would it mean you'd still be here?
Would you then feel real?
Would I then have someone to call, Dad?

The outro is swift, but melancholy. I sit by the piano for a few seconds longer before I turn to face the class, resisting my eyes from getting watery. I'm in disbelief that I managed to play the song from start to finish without stumbling. Just as Lucas knew I could.

All eyes remain on me, including Mr Lennard who looks speechless. Then, far from what I expected, everyone stands up and claps, including Ali. A standing ovation ... Am I still asleep? This weakens my knees, making it difficult to stand.

I glance towards Mr Lennard who fails to keep a poker face. He wipes away at his eyes with a handkerchief and blows his nose afterwards. But what truly grabs my attention is someone else, whose feeble body leans against the classroom door. Her face is red from crying and snot falls from her nose but that doesn't bother her.

"Mum?"

She doesn't stop her tears as she races to where I'm still sitting. My body seems to think it's glued to the chair.

Mum hugs me, rubbing my shoulders, and reminding me how proud I've made her.

"Wynter, that was ... Your dad would have loved hearing your song. And your voice, oh sweetheart. You sing so beautifully, so enchantingly. You really do."

Mum pulls me in even closer to tighten our embrace. When you're a young child, a mother's hug takes away all the pain and makes everything feel okay again. When you're older, a mother's hug is the comfort you still need, but it doesn't erase the pain. At this very moment, I feel like a small child again, rescued by my mother's hug. A feeling I wish to preserve for the rest of my days.

22

Outrun

Stacey stops by our house over the next four days, each time attempting to see if I'm able to talk.

"You're going to have to talk to her again, one day," Ara tells me as I stand in front of our bookshelf. One half of me wants to pick up a book and start reading again, but the other half reminds me that it's not the same without my lunchtime book club member Lucas.

"You don't understand ... She hid a vital truth from me. From all of us."

"To be fair, neither of us will ever understand. I don't think Stacey will, either. Do you honestly believe she told Lucas to go see you with the intention of him being hit by a car?"

I let Ara's words sink in.

"What about this book? It doesn't look touched at all. Although I'm not sure the plot will help with your healing right now." Ara pulls out *Bridge To Terabithia* which was supposed to be mine and Lucas' next TBR book, together. I swallow deeply, whilst also remembering that it was Stacey who recommended it.

Holding the book, I admire its cover and the pages yet to be turned. Before I can convince myself otherwise, I quickly slot the book back in its spot on the shelf, angry at the thought Lucas and I allowed Stacey to influence our TBR list.

"What's really wrong, Wynter?"

"What do you mean?"

"I can understand if you're angry at Stacey right now, I don't blame you. It's only natural to feel some sort of betrayal. But, it's not doing you any good."

"I'm fine."

"No, you're not. I've been keeping my mouth shut because you've needed time to grieve, but I hate seeing you like this, Wynter, you're stuck."

"Stuck?"

"You're stuck in time, thinking Lucas will just miraculously walk through the door."

Ara carries on as I remain silent, "I'm not trying to take away the fact that Lucas will always be your best friend and have a place in your heart. Really, I'm not. But Wynter, you still have people around you who love you, who want to see you happy. We haven't died too. We're still here."

An onset of tears flow from my stinging eyes. "It's not the same. Lucas wasn't supposed to die so soon!"

I ignore whatever Ara has to say and run out the front door.

I run.

And run.

And run.

Ara yells out and starts running after me. Of course, she's the better runner out of the two of us, but today's not the same. I'm outrunning her. For once in my entire existence, I'm ahead of Ara. She continues calling out to me, pleading for me to turn back, but I don't.

It doesn't bother me that I'm still in my pyjamas running around the streets with onlookers. These streets are the pathways that once led Lucas to me.

When I run past Drew's house, he's out the front chasing Rose around their blooming Frangipani tree while Delilah sits gleefully on his shoulders.

"Mini Faye!" he calls out, noticing my state of anguish.

But I keep running. I don't stop. Even as I run past a few familiar faces from school, who burst into a fit of laughter as they witness me in daggy clothes, I don't stop.

I run.

And run.

And run.

Until I outrun Ara that tad bit more and she's no longer trailing behind. She's disappeared from my vicinity. *Maybe running away is my new superpower.* My pace remains constant and my feet start to feel heavy, but they don't require a pit stop. I continue running as though there'll be a *beep* as I make it to the next level, beating my personal best record. Did I just discover the secret to getting to the end of a Beep Test? That anger does the trick. Running uphill, I start to feel my legs giving in, but I surprise myself when I make it to the top.

I run.

And run.

And run.

Until my eyes are so blurry from crying that I'm not sure where my feet have led me to. All the houses look the same, aligned besides the cleanest footpath that sits perfectly along the greenest strip of grass. The only roads I know from memory are the ones I see through the school bus window as it takes me to and from school. Besides that, I can recall the roads Mum takes when she drives us to Westfield. But we haven't been shopping in a while. Even then, these don't look like the same roads that I've been on before. Where am I?

I am braver than I think, stronger than I feel. I have the courage to face my fears.

I recite these words over and over again, yet they fail to spark any sort of relief. There's an overwhelming patch of sadness spreading across my insides.

I am braver than I think, stronger than I feel. I have the courage to face my fears.

My head is spinning which makes it a challenge to stand freely. I can't push back my mental desire to keep running, but my physical state is sabotaging my mission. Every stride feels like I'm trying to lift my feet out of quicksand. My legs are tender and burning as though every muscle is straining.

I am braver than I think, stronger than I feel. I have the courage to face my fears.

But I'm not. I know that now. I'm simply not.

Accepting defeat, I fall to my knees and my pants soak up the wet grass. My breathing becomes rapid as my crying intensifies, so much so that hiccups make themselves known. It hurts to cry.

I glance at the autumn leaves scattered around me. How did I find myself in this situation? How did I go from having rosy outlooks, to failing to recognise the beauty of nature? I reach for a heart-shaped orange leaf and scrunch it in the palm of my hands. Autumn isn't the same without Lucas. These leaves aren't the same. Nothing is the same. He should still be here telling me how damn beautiful these leaves are. But he's not.

In the distance, the sun is blinding, but I forcefully glare at its brightness. Its rays overlook the double storey houses and stretch across the empty roads. Did I think running this far would lead me onto a road back to Lucas? Where I'll fall into the safety of his arms as I cross the finish line? Was this all to try and run away from my innermost fears of letting go? To make myself believe that I can change my own reality? Or was my desperate attempt to run away a lost cause without purpose? Without a destination. All I'm left with is a heavy heart with no answers.

My body starts to shiver and even though there's a sunny patch a few metres away, I stay still. Thoughts start to diminish from my mind. I've lost the race. Whatever this race was.

After several minutes, the still air is disrupted by a car pulling over abruptly. I hear the car door slam shut almost as quickly as it parks, but I don't look up at the figure who steps out.

"Mini Faye! There ya are. I've been driving all over town to find ya." Drew wraps his arms around my shoulder, hushing me from crying.

"It's okay," he says in a gentle voice, the same tone he uses to calm down his daughters. I wonder whether Dad would be able to soothe me if he were alive. I feel like a small child who has fallen over, grazing a thick layer of my skin that exposes its bleeding, and desperately needing the aid of my parents.

"It's okay. You're okay. One sec, let me help ya up." He uses all his strength to lift me and lead me to the car.

The tears are cascading down my face and sniffling makes it hard to breathe.

"Your mum and sister are worried sick 'bout ya. They're searching all across town too."

"Mum's driving?" I choke out, only now realising the seriousness of what I've done.

"Ya bet. Don't worry, I'm gonna call her now so she knows you're safe. I've never seen her so scared before."

I'm not sure I'm ready to go home just yet and face Mum and Ara, who are the only two people left on this planet who love me beyond measure. The only two people, other than Lucas, who care for me not because they have to, but because they choose to.

I've let them down.

"They must hate me ..."

"Far from it. You and Ara have been nothin' but her biggest joy ... Did ya know me and Luna were watching Ara for your parents while Faye was in labour? Your dad wanted to be by her side."

"I only recently found out just how bad Dad's accident was."

"Me and Luna ... we still think, what if we just drove Ara to the hospital instead, y'know? We still kick ourselves for not doin' that."

I recognise a new angle of pain that stems from Dad's accident. I'm suddenly realising the magnitude of regret people can hold from something out of their control. I feel Drew's heartache as though it's still raw.

"Look, Mini Faye. I know I'm just Drew from next door and I'm not the first person you'd run to for advice. But I can spot a broken heart when I see one. I can't imagine what you're going through. I'd be a total wreck if I lost Luna or the twins and I'm what, double ya age? Kid, give yourself some time to grieve and don't feel bad 'bout it. Don't let anyone tell ya there's a right or wrong way to cry. If ya need to run, run. But do it at the park. If ya need to scream, shout. Who cares if ya get stares. Do what ya need to do to let the pain hurt less. But in a controlled setting, yeah? There's a heck of a lot of us who love ya. Be safe."

In all these years I've known Drew, he's always been the nice bloke, the fun dad, the friendly neighbour, but never the one who could bring you back to reality without crushing your soul.

I respond weeping, and he nods, letting me know that he understands without me having to say a single word.

"But one more thing ... Your family ... Don't shut them out. Let them be there for ya, yeah?"

Sitting in the passenger's seat, I draw my knees to my chest and cradle myself. Quivering, my eyes close momentarily as I retrace the events I had just gone through. It takes all of my mental capacity to find the strength to open my eyes again and face what's to come.

After several minutes, the streets start to look familiar. I'm in disbelief at the distance I ran. When the car turns into our street, the first street I recognise clearly with certainty, I can see Mum and Ara waiting outside by our front porch, eagerly waiting for Drew's car. Mum's been through so much already, I shouldn't have added to her list of worries.

They run down the driveway to meet me by the curb as soon as Drew parks. Mum looks like she's aged twenty years in the short amount of time I was gone.

"Wynter!" Mum calls out, running to the car door, opening it for me.

"Wynter, sweetheart." She's crying just as much as I was. "Please don't ever scare us like that again!"

I'm trapped in Mum's embrace, but it makes me feel safe and loved and needed and longed for. I feel at home.

"Thank you, Drew," Mum says whilst turning towards him, without separating from me. "I'm so thankful you found her, someone she knows."

"She zoomed past me. I could tell that ain't something Mini Faye does. Luna's at home with the twins ... Thankfully your girl's all safe and sound now before the rain picks up. Looks like there's a storm comin'. She's a good kid, and a bloody athlete that's for sure."

Mum returns a smile, almost a chuckle at that thought. My lips start to curl too.

Ara stands by Mum, unsure of what to do. There's only been a handful of instances recorded in the hypothetical *Ara's List of Uncertainties* but standing before me in a lost state has never been on that list.

In my heart, I know exactly what I need to do.

Without saying a single word, I walk up to Ara and wrap myself around her. She knows what this hug represents and I'm certain of that because of the way she locks me in her arms, reciprocating the embrace with nothing but love.

Ara knows I love her.

That I need her.

That I'm sorry.

Ara knows, like only a big sister does.

I am braver than I think, stronger than I feel. I have the courage to face my fears.

This time, I believe every single word.

23

Choices

THE DOORBELL CHIMES THE same distinct tune as I remembered. When the door opens, I'm welcomed pleasantly without any hesitation to invite me in.

"Oh, Wynter, darlin', so glad you're here. Come on in, let's get you something warm to drink."

"Thank you, Mrs Jones."

My nerves are intertwined, but deep down I know I'm exactly where I need to be.

"Let's see … We've got some Green tea, Earl Grey, English Breakfast, Hot Cocoa, and … some Jasmine tea. Unless of course you drink coffee?"

"English Breakfast would be nice, thank you."

Mrs Jones hums as she stirs together an English Breakfast tea for the two of us.

"Is Stacey home?" I ask, finally spitting out the question that's been weighing on my mind and the reason for this visit.

"She'll be home soon, darlin', she's just at netball practice. She only recently joined the club down the road. Makes it nice and easy because she can just walk home most days."

"She's so good at sports. She was the last one standing when we did the Beep Test."

"Oh, she really is. But she hasn't been sporty all her life. It's been her way of releasing anger. Let's just say she was a very angry child. Sports helped to calm her. I mean, she still struggles at times, but she's a much happier person now. I can see the difference having seen her actions first-hand"

I realise that you can never really know a person the way you think you do. Stacey has struggles of her own. If I paid closer attention, maybe I could have learned a thing or two about her. But my mind has been semi-absent recently.

I lost Lucas, yes. But the world isn't made up of only me and Lucas. I remind myself of this as I take a sip of my tea.

"I'm sorry about what Stacey did," Mrs Jones says, softening her tone. "I hope there's still some room to rekindle the friendship."

We're interrupted by the sound of the front door opening and footsteps approaching us. Stacey's right, you can hear even the softest footsteps tiptoeing down the marble floors.

"That should be Stacey," Mrs Jones confirms, both nervous and elated.

"Oh boy! Training was exhausting today. Coach didn't let—" Stacey stops mid-sentence realising there's one extra person in the room.

"Wynter?" she says, suddenly disregarding the presence of her mum.

"Mmm, I've got a load of washing to do. I'll be in the laundry room if you need me." Mrs Jones flees the kitchen, giving us both a reassuring smile before disappearing.

Without Mrs Jones I find myself feeling ill in the stomach. The butterflies have quadrupled making sure I'm aware they're well and truly there.

"Hey."

"Hey."

We're both lost for words, Stacey more so than me.

"How are you?" I ask and then quickly regret asking. How is she? Of course, she's not okay.

"Netball training was pretty intense today," Stacey replies, avoiding the question and answering in a roundabout way.

"Stacey, I uh—"

"Don't, Wynter, please. Don't say sorry. It's me who needs to do that."

"I shouldn't have read your messages between you and Lucas. I'm sorry."

"If I could rewind time, I wouldn't have been so pushy. I hate that I get like that sometimes. I get so caught up in making everything seem like a movie, that I forget I'm puppeteering real people."

"I was angry at myself for Lucas' actions, but I'm trying to accept that the reality is, we really can't control what someone else chooses to do. The end choice comes from them. I just wished Lucas chose otherwise that night. We're only a few streets away from each other. It goes to show that there's no guarantee that means nothing bad could happen. Even in a quiet neighbourhood."

"I couldn't sleep after Lucas died. Every day I blamed myself for his death. It took me so much strength to be honest with Mum. The guilt was eating me alive. I was falling into depression at home, even though I tried my best to look fine at school."

"I'm so sorry you went through that."

"When I showed Mum the messages, I could tell she was saddened by it. She had always reminded me about putting less pressure on others, and that no means no, no matter what the situation is. I had failed to remember that, or maybe my subconscious chose not to. But either way, I knew Mum was disappointed. Instead of lecturing me, she held me tight in her arms. How did I deserve that kind of love?"

Stacey's tears stream down her cheek, but she doesn't wipe them away.

"Wynter, I'm truly sorry. I wish I could take back the words I sent to Lucas that night. Erase them. I wish I could have been less scared and told you the truth right away. I wish I could rewrite history. Undo the harm I've caused. And I understand if you can't forgive me."

The room feels smaller somehow, as if the air has been sucked out, leaving us vulnerable.

"I think I've come to realise that this isn't about forgiveness. Stacey, there's nothing to forgive you for because you never did anything wrong in the first place. We're both just trying to understand each other's pain that we both can't figure out ourselves."

Stacey reaches for my hand, shaking slightly. "I can see why Lucas thought the world of you Wynter. Your kindness ..."

"Stacey, we both lost a friend. And maybe our peace of mind somewhere along the way. Maybe neither of us can ever change the past, but we can decide how to move forward."

Stacey looks up, eyes red and puffy with a slight nod, taking in my words.

"Can we maybe start over?" I ask, wiping away at Stacey's tears. "Move forward, together?"

Stacey inhales deeply, steadying her breath. "I'd like that, Wynter. I'd really like that."

The rooms starts to feel bigger—the air is no longer suffocating. Stacey leans in for a hug, holding me tight. In that long hold, I think about how it's not going to be easy, but it's the only way to let go of resentment. Stacey's warmth feels genuine.

As we unlock from each other's arms, we smile thinking about the fresh start to this friendship. I reach for my bag and shuffle its contents.

"What're you looking for?" Stacey asks with a raised brow.

"Here it is," I say as I pull the book out from the bottom of my bag. "I brought this with me."

At this point, Stacey's gasping for air and her breathing is heavy. Her tears remain free-flowing, but this time, her mouth shapes into a thankful twinkle.

"I was thinking," I say, "maybe we can start where Lucas and I last left off? I mean, you *are* a member of our unofficial book club, remember?"

Stacey nods in hysterics, accepting my invitation. She throws her arms around me again, squeezing me for a fierce hug that feels intense and almost overwhelming. But I know that there's no better way for Stacey to show her absolute joy.

"Wynter ... this ... You don't know how much this means to me. Thank you so much. I promise I'll be honest with you from now on."

Holding *Bridge To Terabithia* in her trembling hands, Stacey continues to shower me with eternal gratitude.

Mrs Jones returns, sensing a shift in the atmosphere and offers a gentle smile. She walks over and extends her arms around us both. "Oh how you girls remind me of being young again ..."

Stacey responds with a teasing laugh, but grips her mum's embrace tighter.

As I walk home, I feel a weight lifting. I notice the glittering canopy of stars. The soft rustling of trees. The refreshing chill of the air. The little joys are starting to magnify again.

***

"How did it go?" Ara asks as soon as I walk through our hallway. She's in the middle of watering Mum's plant babies, nurturing them the same way Mum does. It occurs to me that I've failed to recognise their existence lately but glancing at them now sends a calming signal to my brainwaves. It's no wonder they're so precious to Mum.

I choke on my words trying to answer Ara's simple question because recalling what just happened makes me emotional. The emotional roller coaster ride is real. Just when you think it's smooth sailing, you head for a giant slope, struggle to tackle it without stumbling, and then before you know it, before any part of you is ready, you're heading downhill at a speed beyond measure. And then one day, somehow, it's back to smooth sailing.

"We've patched things up," I pause for a moment before continuing to settle my thoughts. "Thanks, Ara. I don't know what I'd do without you."

"Thanks?"

"I know I was mad about it earlier, but you're right. Losing Lucas made me lose myself too, in more ways than one. My focus. It blurred my vision ... A part of me thought I'd have a permanent hole in my heart. But you helped fill that horrible void, Ara. Thank you for never losing sight of me. And for just wanting to help. I see that now."

"You know I'll never stop being here for you. And, not only me. You've got Mum, Lucas' entire family, as well as Drew's, your teachers ... and Stacey."

I smile, convincing myself that I am surrounded by people who care for me too.

"I guess I thought I was strong enough to handle things on my own. To cope alone."

"You *are* strong, Wynter. But being strong doesn't mean you have to endure through all the heartache alone. It takes great strength to seek or accept help. Always remember that."

Ara releases a soft sigh of relief. "Also," she quickly adds with excitement, "I noticed one less book on the bookshelf."

She points at the empty space between her favourite books and her eyes sparkle with anticipation.

"Make sure you tell me as soon as you've finished reading it. We haven't discussed a book in so long. I've missed our conversations."

"Me too," I say, meaning it with full honesty. "I've missed us, too."

And in that brief moment, I feel whole again.

24

Reenactment

The dreaded Drama class isn't so terrible anymore now that there's a voice of reason louder than Ali's. Stacey is outspoken but she knows when to speak to stand up for anyone in Ali's firing line. When she does, it's her words that are raised, not her voice.

Today, we're all presenting our reenactment of a scene from Shakespeare's Macbeth as our way of analysing the play. Mrs Yieldeman thought it would be a clever tie-in with our English class since we have to write an essay about it too.

"Analysing the play to be able to act out the scene you're working on takes a lot of time and effort," Mrs Yieldeman reminds us. "It's no easy feat. But, it'll help you write your essays with a deeper understanding and a lot more conviction to back up what you write."

It makes sense. But I'm not so sure I find acting to be as comforting as writing. At least with the essay, I can describe the emotions the characters endure. With reenacting the scenes, I need to somehow be able to portray and convey the same emotions through movement.

"Alrighty-o!" Mrs Yieldeman grabs everyone's attention. "We're going to mix things up a bit. Now I know you've all been doing so well practising your lines word for word, whilst also trying to remember the actions that go along with them, but today, when you present your reenactments, there'll be no words. The room should be so quiet that I'm able to hear the sound of a pin dropping."

Mrs Yieldeman isn't normally the kind to drop a bombshell as easily as she just did. Instantly my heart is racing and my mind skips to worst-case scenarios. There's no quitting because that would result in an automatic fail and because I'm paired with Stacey, it would impact her score too.

My restlessness becomes obvious because Stacey whispers, "It'll be fine," in my ear.

Mrs Yieldeman approaches us. "You two will be up first. Set the tone for the rest to follow."

If my heart was racing two seconds ago, it's now on the verge of veering off track. I don't know what's more nerve-racking—going first or last. Being the first to perform means not having any other set bars to go by, but being last means waiting in severe agony, especially if it extends to the next day.

"I've never passed an acting project before," I quickly communicate to Stacey. "I thought I'd have a better chance *with* words, but now I'm going to completely flop. I'm so sorry."

Stacey's composure remains confident and far from nervous. She turns to face me and looks me right in the eye as though this is a life or death situation. "Look, Wynter, you've got this. We've got this. No-one in that audience knows what we practised, so no-one knows if we've made a mistake. If you get stuck, just put a sad face on—it'll bound to mean something. It's a Shakespeare play, after all. It's filled with pain."

Stacey's words are comforting but it hasn't slowed down my heart-beat.

"Plus," Stacey adds, "we can only try our best, right? Your best. My best. No-one else's best."

Stacey and I make our way to the front of the class. The floorspace is empty to mimic a stage.

Act Two, Scene Two. In this scene, Macbeth returns from murdering Duncan, alarmed that he heard a noise. I play Macbeth in our reenactment. Lady Macbeth, who Stacey acts out, dismisses his fears and tells him to return the daggers that he had forgotten to leave behind at the crime scene. However, he refuses, so Lady Macbeth goes instead. When she returns to the castle, her hands are bloody but reassures Macbeth that she just needs to wash it off and return to bed so they don't get caught.

This is the scene Stacey and I are assigned. It's not an easy one to pull off because of the dramatic nature it contains. As we stand in front of the class, my anxiety hits the roof and my hands are trembling. Mrs Yieldeman gives us the cue to commence and suddenly, the only sound I can hear is my heartbeat.

I am braver than I think, stronger than I feel. I have the courage to face my fears.

Performing is a fear that I was able to tackle in Music class. In some ways, I had the piano to fall back on if my voice was to fail me. With this reenactment, I'm exposed entirely. There's no turning back. It's a team task. If I stumble, then I bring Stacey along with me. I can't let that happen.

I close my eyes, regain my posture and breathe deeply before I make my first wordless action.

And just like that, Stacey and I are complimenting each other's movements. We exchange expressions that represent fear to reflect the same emotions from the scene. I didn't realise until now how comforting Stacey is. She makes it less daunting as we continue to replicate the scene. Stacey is gracious and reenacts each movement with purpose. My shyness gets in the way a couple of times, but she helps me carry on and looks past it. After several minutes that felt like an eternity, we are done. We made it through the scene.

Mrs Yieldeman, along with the rest of the class, claps in encouragement as we return to our seats.

"That was brilliant! Well done girls." Mrs Yieldeman smiles from ear-to-ear.

"Next we have ... Let's see. Ali and Lea."

Poised, the pair make their way to the make-shift centre stage. Theirs is Act Three, Scene Two. Without a shadow of a doubt, they reenact the scene perfectly—an A+ performance. Their expressions, especially Ali's, are on point and they don't miss a single emotion to convey. Once their performance is finished, Lea walks back to her seat.

Ali doesn't move which baffles us all.

"Ali, you can take your seat now," Mrs Yieldeman reminds her.

Ali's expression is almost as though she's about to partake in the next scene, but she's alone. Her usual resting face which belongs on *Mean Girls* is absent. To everyone's disbelief, Ali doesn't budge. Instead, she opens an envelope that she retrieves from a nearby desk.

Ali coughs gently to clear her throat. "Dear Future Me, Ali," she says.

The entire class, including Mrs Yieldeman, are quiet and confused. What's going on? This isn't part of today's task. The puzzled faces travel across the room but Ali ignores them and carries on.

"Dear Future Me, Ali. This is supposed to be a letter to my future self so that at the end of the year, I can re-read it and jump for joy because of all the things I've achieved throughout this school year. But I hate who I've become and I'm not sure there's any way to turn back time and fix things. I'm broken.

"Everyone has genuine loyal friends. What do I have? Loyal friends because I force them to be. It wasn't always the case. I once had a friend who I confided in with everything. Who accepted me for my imperfections. Who looked past my moments of weakness. That all changed because of my need to feel better about myself, in all the wrong ways possible.

"Red. Why Red? Because I was teased by Wren, the boy I had a crush on in Year 5 when he found out Wynter got her period before me. Somehow, she was a 'woman' in his eyes. It didn't make any sense. He joined along when everyone chanted 'Red' towards her, so I joined in, trying to impress the boy I liked.

"I wish I could turn back time and not be so blinded and distracted by a crush. It ruined a friendship that would have been long-lasting between Wynter and I. All because I liked a boy.

"I can't change the past but I hope I have the courage to shape a better tomorrow. Each time I try, the social pressure gets to me, and I'm back to being my old cruel self. I hate it. If there's one thing I hope to have achieved by the end of this school year, it's to rekindle a flame I once burnt out on purpose. That person deserves kindness.

"From your current self, Ali."

Mrs Yieldeman is speechless and stunned. But Ali's not done yet. She clears her throat once more before speaking with direct eye contact towards me.

"Wynter ... I'm sorry for being a horrible ex-best-friend. Lucas was lucky to have found you."

My natural reaction is to give Ali a reassuring nod, but my brain is scanning thousands of thoughts in that split second. I know what I have to do, but I need a minute to process it all.

Ali shifts her attention to Mrs Yieldeman. "And Mrs Yieldeman ... I'm sorry for being insensitive. You would have been the most caring mother to baby Kelsie. You're the light and mother-figure most of us need in our day. I'm sorry for hurting you."

Mrs Yieldeman is left in tears—tears that she's probably been holding in for a long time now. It's an apology she needed. She sniffles and nods towards Ali, thanking her with a big bear hug. A hug that Ali probably needed just as equally.

Stacey nudges me, but I'm frozen. I'm still processing what has just taken place.

Lea and Ivy are laughing at Ali from their seats, declaring their new social status. What a turn of events. Lea instructs Ivy to put her backpack on the empty seat that was once Ali's, rising to the title of 'Queen Bee'.

This phases Ali slightly and she's unsure where to wander off to. Instead, Stacey holds her by the hand and welcomes her to sit with us.

I'm still frozen. It feels like an out-of-body experience.

It's been years of hurt, my body doesn't know the right way to respond. I spend the rest of the period trying to navigate through my thoughts and figure out what to do. I fail to pay attention to the rest of the reenactments because my mind keeps wandering. In the corner of my mind I know I've forgiven Ali long ago despite her nastiness. I know that deep down, despite what her actions show, she's always been the same Ali who couldn't hurt a fly. Hurting others all this time was probably hurting her more. It wasn't her.

I look her in the eye and smile the familiar smile she had known from all those many years ago. The smile she returns is nostalgic but authentic.

Ali's back.

25

Salt

I KEEP REPLAYING LUCAS' words, *'I take it now's not a good time to talk?'* It's a thought I can't seem to shake off and it's been crossing my mind whenever there's any moment of quietness. But it remains a mystery now. An unsolved mystery. Even if I attempt to guess, I'll never know, because the one person who can answer it is no longer here. This is the thought I wake up to.

It's a warmer autumn's day which makes it slightly easier to rise from my bed on a Sunday morning. Peering through the window, I admire the birds soaring across clear blue skies with blotches of white clouds scattered throughout. Mr Knox is mowing the front lawn, as scheduled. His routine is somewhat comforting now. Every Sunday morning, he's there and my day starts with a friendly wave from afar. He's never been one to use words often, but he never fails to wave hello.

Mum knocks on my door, slowly opening to peep in.

"Good morning, sweetie."

She sits on my bed, motioning for me to join her.

"You know," she begins, "that wave you return, it makes Mr Knox's day. The smile on his face, it reminds me of when his wife was still here. When he always wore a smile."

"I wish I could remember more about her. It sounds like she was a really nice person."

"She sure was. They spent every morning eating breakfast together on their front porch, watching the moon fade. They never missed a single sunrise."

"That sounds like something straight out of a movie."

"The sound of her laughter. It was contagious. He made her laugh so often. He was the light that centred her universe. And she was his."

Mum leans in closer. "When she died, the air grew cold and the laughter you could recognise from miles away grew silent. For a long while, there was a deep hole in Mr Knox's heart."

I know the feeling of having a deep, endless hole in your heart. A sinkhole.

"I guess what I'm trying to tell you, sweetie, is that it's okay to feel the way you do. And it will take time to start to feel yourself again."

Mum squeezes my shoulders and kisses my forehead.

"I'm heading to the shops for a grocery run, did you want to come?"

"Thanks, Mum, but I think there's someone who's been needing my affection ... I need to attend to him." My lips arch.

"It's good to see you smile, sweetie. I'll be back by lunchtime."

Mum blows me a kiss the same way she used to when I was little, before closing the door behind her. I stare at my reflection on the window. *I am braver than I think, stronger than I feel. I have the courage to face my fears.*

When I head downstairs, I'm welcomed by a new array of indoor plants. Some I recognise by name, like the Zanzibar, Fiddle Leaf and Philodendron Birkin. There's another one planted in a blue-glazed pot but I'm unsure of its kind. The small cluster of leaves reminds me of miniature lily pads held together by one stem. Ara would know the name; the scientific name to be exact.

Pepper wags his tail and shadows my every move.

"There you are, my little shadow. I've missed you. Sorry for not giving you the attention I used to."

Pepper continues wagging his tail, running circles around me.

Today's the day I change the lack of attention I've given him. It's unfair for him to endure the same feeling of loneliness that part of me has gone through recently. It's not easy getting through each day without hearing Lucas' voice and how he can so effortlessly string words together to make me laugh. Maybe just like Mrs Knox, my laugh was contagious to someone else, too.

"Let's go, Pepper. Come on ... Time for a walk."

Pepper waddles towards me, wagging his tail with excitement. As soon as I'm holding his leash he knows that adventure awaits him.

I leave a message for Mum on a Post-it note in case she arrives home from shopping before me: *Taking Pepper for a walk. Be back soon* so that she knows I haven't disappeared. There's no need to sign off with my name because she can tell mine and Ara's handwriting apart without second-guessing.

It'll probably make her happy knowing I'm doing something that is 'normal' again, without Lucas. You don't realise how much someone impacts your life to the extent that they do, until they're gone. But taking any step to crawl out from the sorrows is a big step. No matter how insignificant it may seem, I've learned that any step is *a step*.

As Pepper leads the way, he pulls towards the direction he wants to take. It's ingrained in him to turn left from our driveway knowing with certainty that the footpath will lead us to a nearby park. As we turn left, I'm reminded of the pavement leading to a different point. These blocks of cement that stretch out into the distance are the same pathways Lucas and I would always take.

Lucas loved taking Pepper on walks with me and it was the most exercise we both got.

"Pepper's such a funny little dog. He waddles," Lucas says as he holds the leash tightly, making sure Pepper stays on the footpath. For a small dog, he has a lot of strength.

"He's a rescue dog. The waddle is what drew us to him. He's not like any other sausage dog, he's our little Pepper."

"Do you think about whether he sometimes longs for a friend? A dog friend. The way we humans need human interaction."

"Honestly, it hasn't crossed my mind. I guess I've been so loved up by him, I didn't think he'd need anything more. He's one spoilt little dog."

"Could you imagine being alone? Like, without a single person to talk to each day? Or to just see. I wonder how that would feel like. We're so used to being surrounded by civilisation."

"A bit like the show, Alone? I mean, I can survive being alone at school during lunchtimes, but being completely isolated is something else." I take a moment to reflect on that. "I think I wouldn't last a day on that show, out there misplaced somewhere in the wilderness. It would feel so lonely after a couple of hours of feeling the calmness. I'd miss home way too easily. I'm certain I'd be the first contestant to tap out."

"If Pepper could talk, I wonder what he'd say. I mean don't get me wrong, he's beyond happy being a part of your family, but I do wonder whether dogs, in general, crave for a dog friend, you know ... to see every

day. Not just the occasional dog friend at the park. But one they build a close relationship with."

"Well maybe one day you can become a dog-dad and your dog and Pepper can be the best of friends. Just like us."

We laugh but take several seconds to let that idea sink in. It's not a half-bad idea.

Pepper spots a Monarch butterfly and starts barking playfully trying to follow its every flutter. With the warmer weather, he's finally seen one again.

As Pepper remains distracted, pouncing around the butterfly, I spot a familiar silhouette approaching us. At first glance, it's as though a figment of my imagination has turned back time to the days Lucas would meet us halfway to the park. His figure is unmistakable, especially when his hair is styled upwards.

It's Guy, but he's not alone.

"What a pleasant surprise," I say as we walk towards each other, bridging the gap that separated us. "It's good to see you."

Guy leans in for a hug and then reinforces a positive and hopeful expression. "Some days are harder than others," he confesses. "But I've got this little fuzzball to keep me company now. She knew the right time to walk into our lives."

"She's so adorable!" My eyes are fixated on the little ball of fluff that hides behind Guy's legs.

"Hello little one ... It's okay." I crouch down to her level and offer my hand. "It's okay," I repeat until her sweet little paws fall before Guy's feet, where she sits still.

"She kept waiting by our doorstep every morning over the last couple of days. She didn't have a collar or microchip and no-one claimed her as theirs after knocking on every door in the neighbourhood. So we decided to keep her. We felt it was a good enough sign that she chose us to be her family. Her fur-ever home." Guy laughs at his own pun.

"She's perfect."

"Lucas would think so too. The number of times he asked Mum and Dad for a dog with white fur. And yes, white fur specifically."

"Was there a method to his madness at least?"

"Well, I guess I should introduce you to our little fuzzball." Guy picks up the little Maltese and cradles her like a baby. "Meet Salt. Lucas always wanted to name our future family dog Salt, so it only made sense to. In hindsight, I just realised why he wanted it to have white fur. Salt. White. Of course."

And then it hits me.

Guy notices my moment of silence as I register the information I've just learned.

"I'm sorry, it's hard for me to talk about Lucas sometimes too. I shouldn't have assumed you were ready—"

"No, it's okay. It's just that ... Well, I guess I should introduce you to our little waddling dog. Meet Pepper."

Guy immediately puts the two and two together and smiles. "Ah, of course. Only Lucas would think of a fitting name to go along with it. Well, it looks like Pepper has a forever fur friend named Salt now. Salt and Pepper."

We both laugh.

Even when Lucas has left us with a hole in our hearts, he still manages to make us laugh.

When Guy puts Salt back on the ground, she runs towards Pepper and greets him with a sniff to his behind. Guy and I laugh louder until the laughter turns into tears.

Happy tears.

26

Antidote

ALI HAS NEVER BEEN one to read books and enjoy them. She says she reads them to fall asleep. When people say they're not a reader, to me, they just haven't found the right book yet to get them started. There'll be that one book that changes your mind about books and it's so personal that you just never know which story will touch your heart, until it captures you on a road to no return.

Stacey and I are already halfway through *Bridge To Terabithia* and she's right. It's so well written and I find myself turning the pages, one after another, constantly. If lunchtime was longer, I'd be finished reading it by now.

This time is slightly different though. I don't open my novel right away because Ali's sitting with us and I don't want her to feel uncomfortable. She's already taken a huge hit in the social status ladder. The best thing Stacey and I can do for her is to show our appreciation.

"So, Ali," Stacey breaks the silence. "Since you've joined our unofficial book club, any books you want to add to our TBR list?"

"What's a TBR list?" Ali asks as her cheeks blush two tones brighter.

Stacey looks at me as though I've forgotten to share crucial information with her.

"Um yeah, so, Ali's not much of a reader," I say. "But realistically we don't have to spend the whole lunchtime reading. If there aren't any book club rules, then there aren't any to break, right?"

"I prefer watching movies. It takes two hours versus two weeks to finish it," Ali explains. "But I don't want to intrude on your little book club. Just pretend I'm not here and do what you'd normally do."

"But you *are* here, Ali," I shoot back. "So we're not going to just ignore you. Remember, invisibility is *my* superpower."

Ali remembers. Reminding her of my superpower makes her eyes watery. Sometimes memories have the ability to trigger waterworks without warning. Ali quickly realises this.

"I can't believe mine was flying. So unoriginal," Ali regrets.

"Well, if you ever want to add anything to our TBR list, our *To Be Read* list I mean, just let us know. Even if it's a book you've considered reading but are unsure of."

Ali pulls out a book from her bag and then laughs. "What about this? I need to read it for English class. Maybe it'll help me understand it better if I had two helpful bookworms?"

Stacey and I nod and within an instant, Stacey's adding *Little Women* to the list.

"Thank you," Ali says.

"This better be the book that changes your life," Stacey and I both tease.

Ali's grin is interrupted by the presence of Lea and Ivy who purposely walk our way. Their arms are linked and they stride in unison making it a mission to make their existence known.

"I can't believe I walked around school looking like that," Ali says whilst covering her face with the palm of her hand, embarrassed.

"Hopefully one day, they'll come around too," I say, knowing that a part of Ali probably misses Lea and Ivy. Despite their tough exterior, they still have a heart, and maybe Ali was able to witness their kindness perhaps behind closed doors. But I can understand that they've built an idea of themselves in front of everyone at school—it would be hard to change that into something less than.

Lea makes a conscious effort to look Ali in the eye and then whispers into Ivy's ear. They both walk away, chuckling. They're living up to their villain titles.

"I was certain Lea would be on top one day," Ali says with an undertone. "She was obsessed with popularity. From what Ivy told me in secret, Lea was always coming in at second. She'd be crowned the runner-up. The finalist. She would miss out by one. It's quite sad actually."

"And it doesn't help that it's hard enough being a teenager," Stacey chimes in.

"Well," I add my two cents in. "We're not alone. I mean look at us, our book club is so popular it's a book club of three now."

If Lucas was still here, his face would be beaming with joy. He knows I'm not one to easily open my heart and let my guard down. But look at me now. I have not one, but two friends sitting with me.

In these short glimpses of laughter, I find myself feeling less guilty of smiling. In my heart, I know that Lucas would have wanted to see me smiling daily. Instead of forcing myself to move forward a certain way, I'm allowing time to lessen the pain. I'm expecting the pain will come and go and I'll need a top-up of my own formulated medicine from time to time. Mum and Ara, and now Ali and Stacey too, are the antidotes to those down days. The days when negative thoughts flood my mind and I start to blame myself again for Lucas' final breath.

Ali and Stacey are the antidotes I never knew I needed. But here they are, reminding me that it's okay to smile again, to be reading again, to have a friend again, and to have thoughts other than a memory of a lost friend.

The pain of losing Lucas is less suffocating when I have these daily reminders. Even seeing Guy more often as we cross paths at school aches my heart a little less now. I try my best to see Guy for Guy, not Guy for his younger brother who once existed and looked like his twin.

As my mind crosses Guy, I'm momentarily confused by my thoughts and reality because there's a shadow mounting over me that interrupts my chain of thoughts. A silhouette that once mirrored Lucas'. Guy stands relaxed, with a few of his friends waiting nearby.

"Hey, Wynter. I'll be quick," Guy says, aware of the time.

"Hey." I stretch up so that I'm standing now too. My legs feel slightly numb from sitting crossed-legged for so long.

"If you're free after school this arvo, did you want to take Pepper for a walk? We can meet halfway? I'll bring Salt."

"Uh ..." I struggle to construct a few words together even though the question is far from complicated to answer.

Guy saves me from the lingering silence. "Wynter, I hope you don't feel as though I'm trying to be friends as a way to replace Lucas. I'm not, I'm really not. It's just that, no-one else knew him the way you did. It's comforting."

"Sometimes I find it difficult just looking at you. You look so much like Lucas."

"Imagine having to see yourself in the mirror every day and seeing a reflection of your brother. I still struggle too. And even though they deny it, I know it pains Mum and Dad too. They see Lucas every time they look at me."

"I'm sorry," I say. "Sometimes I get so buried in my thoughts, I forget how others feel about Lucas' death."

"Don't be, we all heal differently. But, maybe ... *maybe* it wouldn't hurt to go for a walk later? I'm sure you've missed Salt."

I think about it for a moment and how refreshing it was to see Guy with Salt yesterday. Salt must be a gift Lucas left behind because she's too adorable to frown around.

"Around 4pm?" I ask.

"Around 4pm it is," Guy replies. His mouth arches the same way Lucas' always did. Guy *isn't* Lucas, I mentally remind myself. I need to remember that.

27

Envelope

M RS YIELDEMAN'S EYES ARE beaming as she witnesses me, Stacey and Ali working peacefully together. She continues gliding on her tiptoes monitoring the groups scattered around the classroom. Once she's done her rounds, she approaches our group again and places the palm of her hand on my shoulder.

"Wynter, I'd like to speak with you after class please," she says. Her eyes are still glowing with kindness. It's hard to believe this woman has been through so much heartache with the friendly smile she displays each day. I wonder if I'll be like her one day.

Stacey and Ali give me the 'uh-oh' look assuming that what Mrs Yieldeman has said is to do with my classwork. Most of my peers get the gist of things whenever our class teacher approaches me with those words. Even Mum has had to use that on me. Generally, it means I've failed a test, I need to work harder to pass the class in general, or I have to do extra work to catch up to the rest of the class.

Right now, it's probably to do with my Macbeth performance. If there was a mirror in front of me during the reenactment, so that I could see what everyone else could see, then I'd most likely be wanting to speak to me too after class if I was the teacher. But if I failed that performance, then it means Stacey did too.

I feel light-headed knowing there's a possibility that my performance wasn't good enough, and as a result, Stacey's overall mark will be brought down too. I glance at the clock, which shows that there are still another ten minutes until the bell rings. Ten whole minutes sitting here in agony and wondering where I went wrong.

And then a thought crosses my mind. What if there *isn't* anything wrong and for the first time I'll experience receiving good news from the teacher? Something like, *"You passed that task with flying colours. Keep it up."*

It's hard to imagine that being the case because usually I'd at least have some sort of inkling about doing well. And even then, it would just be a *"You just passed, well done,"* type of comment.

As the minutes tick away slowly, Ali and Stacey have their speculations. This side-tracks us from completing the group task we're supposed to be working on.

"Maybe Mrs Yieldeman is giving you an early look into your test scores," Stacey guesses.

"Or maybe it's got nothing to do with Drama class," Ali adds.

"Thinking hurts my brain," I whine.

"The bell will ring any minute now. But you have to tell us all about it afterwards," Stacey says in excitement.

"Even if it's to do with me failing? Or doing so horribly bad in class that I'll be forced to have tutoring during the school holidays?" I say to get Stacey less excited.

Waiting for the final minute to pass feels like sitting at the doctor's office, anxiously waiting for a diagnosis.

Tick tock.

The sound of the clock ticking lingers and somehow each tick sounds like it's moving slower.

A few heartbeats later, the bell rings. It leaves a ringing sound in my ear long after it's stopped.

"Good luck," both Ali and Stacey say before they leave the room.

Mrs Yieldeman motions for me to stay behind even though every living cell in my body is aware of that request.

"Take a seat, Wynter."

I do as directed, still unaware of what this impromptu meeting holds.

"Wynter, I've been um and ahing about this for a while. I'm not sure if it's the best thing to do, but I keep coming back to convince myself it is."

I knew it. She's going to fail me in her class. The one class that everyone calls a breeze.

"I'm sorry in advance if it turns out that it wasn't the best thing to do, but I'm trusting my gut on this."

"It's okay, Mrs Yieldeman. It's not your fault, I'm just hopeless at acting. With or without words."

Mrs Yieldeman is puzzled and attempts to rephrase her words. "Wynter, dear. This has nothing to do with your acting skills or lack thereof. It's to do with this."

In front of me lies a white envelope, face down. My heart sinks with no anchor to keep it afloat. I recognise the envelope without needing any confirmation but it's only when Mrs Yieldeman turns it the right way around that my mind registers what's happening and it feels like shrapnels have flown their way towards me.

"In all honesty, this has been sitting in my top drawer ever since Lucas died. I phoned Mr and Mrs Mensah and they wanted you to have it."

"I—Mrs Yieldeman ..." I hold the envelope and tears start to build up in my eyes. My vision becomes unclear, just as my heart continues to feel weighed down.

Lucas wasn't in my Drama class but he still had Mrs Yieldeman as his Drama teacher. Staring at this envelope marked with Lucas' name on the front in his messy handwriting validates that he did the same task as me.

I breathe deeply, hands shaking, and tears now dropping from my chin.

"I've been waiting for the right time to give it to you, but I realise we all have a different 'right time' and the longer I wait, the longer it sits here collecting dust."

"I don't know what to say," I choke out.

"You don't have to say anything. But please, take it. It belongs safely in your hands. No-one else's."

***

The bus ride home feels a little different today. A small part of Lucas is nestled safely in my bag and not knowing what's written on the pages is daunting.

When the bus stops, Arti gives me a comforting nod. I nod back as quickly as I can so that he knows I'll be okay.

My heart pumps when I reach our front door and realise that on the one hand, I'll soon be reading into Lucas' most inner thoughts but on the other hand, maybe it's not as drastic as I expect them to be.

Using a metal letter opener, the envelope rips open in one swift, but precise motion. With trembling hands, I unfold the page and analyse the messy handwriting that many would think was some sort of Morse code that needed to be cracked. There's no denying this is Lucas' script.

I take a moment to Box Breathe and then I put my full focus on the words.

Dear Future Lucas,

It's present-day Lucas here! How am I? The same old, really. This is an interesting task and I'm actually looking forward to reading this at the end of the school year, but everyone will probably think lamely of me ... even more.

There's nothing overly exciting about my day to day BUT woohoo, my Music performance is underway. I just need to practise it a few more times and then record a copy for Wynter.

Wynter. I feel like she deserves a mention in my future me letter because I know she'll be there. One year from now, five years from now, even twenty years from now, she'll be there. I'm 100% certain. And so when I read this at the end of the year, I can say with full confidence that Wynter will be next to me reading (and laughing) along.

But of course, there'll be a new addition to our small friendship circle because I can promise Pepper (yes, I'm making a promise to a dog) that he'll have his own dog best friend soon too. Now how to make that happen ... Because the dog NEEDS to be named Salt. I'm saving up my allowance to afford one. I really should talk to Wynter about this grand plan though, to let her know it's really happening and not just an idea. I'll try talking to her at the bus stop.

Stacey's family are in Sydney now too. I do hope she and Wynter get along. I mean, behind the shy front Stacey can be very upfront and Wynter's a little more soft-spoken, but I don't think friends are supposed to be identical in everything, otherwise, it would be a constant clash after clash.

Okay, so I just tried reading what I've written so far and wow, my handwriting is shocking. At least no-one will be able to decipher these words if this letter was to ever get lost. Well, except for Wynter. She can somehow read my illegible handwriting.

Apart from what I've written, I don't have any set plans for the year. I kind of just go along with the flow of things. Not sure if that's smart or just a lazy approach. Either way, I'm at least looking forward to getting my L plates soon. I've heard everyone passes the test first go. I still need to work on convincing my parents to let me drive their car to practise. I can't afford proper driving lessons yet. I guess there's no real rush to be driving anyway, since I'll always be accompanied by an adult. It's not like I can just go on a road trip and visit every library and bookstore around town without a chaperone. One day ... And then Wynter and I can take turns driving around Australia on a grand book club adventure. Trust me, it sounds better than it ... I mean it'll be better than it sounds.

Well, adios, for now, present me. Hopefully future me still finds you funny.

From present funny,
Lucas.

Yes, Lucas, you'll never stop being funny, especially in my eyes. The kind of funny that makes even the saddest heart have a glimmer of hope. The kind of funny that stops people in their tracks to take a moment to let joy take part in their day. The kind of funny that makes a frail old woman or a quiet little toddler burst into tears of laughter. The kind of funny that makes the shy unnamed bookworm sitting all alone find a reason to feel seen in a busy world where no-one else stops to check in on the ones who are falling through the cracks.

As I fold the letter back up, along the same creases Lucas did, I feel thankful and reflect on the friendship we had. *It's okay to smile,* I remind myself. So I do. And the smile carries on because I realise I was able to share and hold onto so many wonderful memories with Lucas. As Miss Xi once reminded me, memories are good. They're there when you need a little pick me up. I just need to search through my memory bank because I'll surely find one where Lucas has made me laugh. So much so that my jaws hurt from smiling.

28

Next Time

"**S**ORRY, WE'RE A LITTLE late," I say, tugging Pepper along.

Salt pulls along the leash Guy's holding and makes her way straight to Pepper, greeting him as though they haven't seen each other in a year.

"Looks like they're already enjoying each other's company," Guy says.

"Makes it easier taking them on walks together."

"Until they have their first disagreement," Guy jokes.

Separating Lucas from Guy is harder than I thought. The more Guy speaks, the more I'm reminded of Lucas. They have the same waves in their voices. The way they accentuate certain words. The way their R's roll off their tongue. The way they pause at certain points. It's a reality I need to get used to, especially if Salt and Pepper have future walks together lined up.

"Mrs Yieldeman gave me this today, it's the reason why we were a bit late."

"A letter?"

"Lucas'."

"I never knew he was one to write letters, to be honest."

"It was a task Mrs Yieldeman asked for us to do. A letter to our future selves."

"Oh, right …" Guy pauses, unsure whether to ask me if I'm okay or whether he should assume I'm not.

"When she gave it to me, my heart stopped. I didn't think I'd be able to handle reading a letter Lucas left behind. And to read about his thoughts for the future. I was afraid I'd read something that I would want to erase from my mind, permanently."

"Lucas talked about his future a lot. He was excited for the years to come. High school wasn't the highlight of his years. He said he knew it was just a small detour to bigger things."

"We wanted to travel around the world, visiting every bookstore and library we could find. We've only ticked the local ones off our list."

"That's still something. A start."

"You think I should keep going?"

Guy looks at me confused. "You mean, you weren't going to?"

"Without Lucas … it … I don't think it will be the same."

"I don't think anything will ever feel the same without him, but we have to keep living. Wake up each morning to live, not just to exist. Lucas replayed that in his and my mind quite often."

"Maybe one day."

"One day at a time, hey?"

"I guess so. One day at a time."

We let that thought dwell in our minds for a few minutes. Salt and Pepper are walking side by side without a fuss, occasionally taking a short break to chase their tails.

"How do you feel after reading his letter?"

"It made me smile. I haven't smiled without feeling a grain of guilt in a while. It was refreshing."

"Even his messy handwriting can make you smile?"

"Yes," I laugh. "He's lucky I could read it."

Guy's dimples dent both cheeks, stamping an image of Lucas' messy handwriting in his mind. "When we were younger, we used to play Doctors. Lucas would choose to be the Doctor but back then he used to just draw scribbles because he didn't know how to write words yet. Mum used to say his handwriting was perfect for a Doctor."

"He would have been a good one if that's the career he chose. Maybe a paediatrician because he's so gentle with children."

"And he had so much patience."

"Yes, that too. No wonder why he was able to be friends with me for so long."

"Yes, that too," Guy teases. "I mean, I'm doing pretty well right, being patient and all?"

I laugh. "You need to work on patience if you're already asking about it."

"You don't say," Guy recites. "You don't say."

Salt pulls Guy along as the jingle of an ice-cream truck blasts from a large speaker, leaving Pepper and I behind.

I start laughing as I witness a small Maltese pulling along Guy. His face matches the colour of the red stop sign as embarrassment takes over. My laugh escalates when Guy looks back, mouthing *help*. On cue, Pepper chases after Salt, and now I'm finding myself in the same predicament as Guy. As soon as he notices, he's laughing just as much as I am.

It's only when both Salt and Pepper reach the ice-cream truck that they decide to stop, giving me a chance to catch up to my breath.

"I forgot to mention," I say, breathing heavily, "I'm super unfit."

"To be fair, my own dog outran me," Guy says, covering his face. "A *Maltese* outran me."

Salt and Pepper bark towards the ice-cream truck, reminding us why we ran here in the first place.

"I'm not so sure about you two," I say whilst looking at the two culprits who are now giving me the sweetest puppy dog eyes. "But Guy and I deserve one for sure."

"My shout," Guy says, pulling out his wallet from his back pocket.

"Thanks, but next time I'll shout. I don't have any cash on me at the moment."

"Sounds like a plan. I like the ring to *next time*."

We sit by a park bench, with an ice-cream held in one hand and a dog leash in the other. The rainbow sprinkles on the top of my soft serve are reminiscent of the different colours Lucas shared with me.

Blue, when he was feeling down, but didn't shy away his sadness from the world, so that I'd be there, a shoulder to lean on. He wasn't ashamed of crying, something I wish I could imitate. His tears were pure and genuine.

Red, which served as a warning, a siren to signal 'stay away, not today'. It was rare, but on these days, Lucas was able to spiral out of whatever evoked him to feel anger. He never went to bed angry. He had the need to fix issues before the sun disappeared for the day.

Green, to reflect his love for nature and his ability to soak in all of its beauty, even if it's just admiring Mr Knox's perfectly mowed bright green lawn. Lucas didn't have a green thumb, but that didn't stop him from appreciating every plant and flower in all their natural state. Mum liked how he noticed whenever there was a new indoor plant placed in her forever-growing collection.

Yellow, the colour of his smile, his laughter, his dimples. Yellow radiates a glow from his eyes. Whenever he smiled, it was hard not to smile in return. His laugh was contagious, just as Mrs Knox's was to everyone else. The warmth of his aura is something I'll forever remember as comfort.

Pink, symbolising his kind and delicate heart. It's hard to imagine how a heart can intertwine with every other heart it meets, but that's the kind of heart Lucas had. One that was filled with love for everyone he met—there was room for others, it didn't matter who. The beating of his heart was in tune with mine, a forever friend.

Orange, because Lucas left a bright and harmonious light in his tracks. Wherever Lucas is, a ray of sunshine was sure to be there, followed by a breathtaking sunset. He's all shades of orange, in its many wondrous ways.

And white, I often think the depth of Lucas is that of a blank canvas. The white is the foundation that shapes him, that encompasses every being that he is. Without this canvas, the colours sprinkled on top wouldn't be as magical as they are.

Guy looks intently at me, mesmerised by my deep thought.

"Your ice-cream's going to melt. What's on your mind?"

"The sprinkles. They remind me of Lucas."

"That's good. Keep remembering him. Every little thing about him."

"I don't even have to try. He sneaks up in my memories every day. I'm so scared that one day it won't be so easy to remember, though."

"One day at a time, remember? Plus, if this ice-cream truck comes around every time we go for walks, I'm sure the memory of sprinkles will be glued to your brain."

We both smile at that thought.

29

The Last Time

Two Years Later: 2017

I STAND IN FRONT of the bathroom mirror, ready for today.

I am braver than I think, stronger than I feel. I have the courage to face my fears.

Stacey and Ali are waiting for me downstairs. Mum wants to take photos of the three of us together before we all head to school for our final day of Year 12. She says it's too chaotic once we enter the school gates and it'll be impossible for her to snap photos of us then.

That's right. It's been two entire years without Lucas. He's not going to be sitting besides me as we wait for our names to be called and walk on stage as we collect our Graduation certificates. It's still difficult to go through events without him but it's in these moments I dig hard to unlock a happy memory we shared instead of drowning in heartache.

I've been dropping by Miss Xi's office weekly. Conversations with her have stemmed from being just about Lucas, to being able to move forward with life without him and not feeling saddened by that. Her weekly reminders help whenever I start to miss Lucas' presence. My heart is still healing from the loss, but I've gained many new friendships. They're not a replacement for Lucas, but an addition to my life.

"Hurry girls," Mum says from the kitchen. "Over here by the Monstera and Lady Palm, it'll pop in the photo."

Ara laughs from the other end of the room, reminiscing her graduation and how over-the-top Mum was for that too.

Stacey and Ali quickly follow Mum's orders as though they're still in Maths class.

"Move five centimetres to the right Stacey please, and oh, Ali, maybe turn your body slightly."

They'd be good models given they've adjusted to Mum's every request without complaining.

"Okay, now, three ... two ... one ... Oh wait, Wynter sweetie, just bring yourself a tad bit closer to Ali, there's a two-centimetre gap that looks off ... Yes, perfect, stop. That looks perfect! Three ... two ... one ... Say cheese!"

"Cheese!" we say altogether as though we're taking a kindergarten class photo. This makes us laugh afterwards and I notice Ara capturing a stolen shot. Mum isn't one to take photos that aren't carefully planned out, but Ara learned from Photography class that sometimes the unexpected ones are the ones that turn out the best. And in this case, it does. Because her Polaroid prints out the photo instantly, and it's perfect. All our eyes are closed from laughter, and our mouths are wide open as though we're hungry lions waiting to be fed, but we look happy and it captures this memory sublimely.

I mouth *thank you* to Ara and she returns a *you're welcome*.

***

There isn't a single empty seat in the school hall. Mr Lee stands on the stage and welcomes everyone to our Graduation assembly. One by one, we walk up on stage as he announces our names. Mrs Yieldeman, our now Year Advisor, joins us by shaking our hand before rewarding us with the certificate. She's gleaming beyond measure and this expression is switched on the entire time. Her tears are held back, although we all know they'll burst straight after the assembly once the spotlight isn't on her. She truly is proud of each one of us graduating today.

Lea and Ivy receive their certificates accompanied by a chant of congratulations in the crowd. Whilst they're still on a pedestal and loving every second of the popularity, I still hope for the day they'll see the world through less nasty eyes. Mum says sometimes the pressure of high school can get to even the kindest of people if they fall into the wrong crowd or idea of what it means to be liked by others.

"And now," Mrs Yieldeman says excitedly into the microphone, "Matilda Walters, our School Dux, has kindly requested for her speech slot to be presented by another student."

The audience is surprised and I can see people whispering amongst themselves wondering why. Matilda is sitting on the stage besides the School Captains and Principal. She smiles at Mrs Yieldeman and gives her the nod of approval to carry on.

"And so, I would like to invite a student onto the stage who, although didn't receive the Dux title, surpassed a devastating and challenging time over the last two years. Despite this, hard work and determination have led her to receive the Proxime Accessit title. Miss Wynter Hope will now present her speech to the student body of the Class of 2017."

I adjust my graduation robe as I stand. Although no-one can see, my nerves linger throughout and my palms start to feel sweaty. With every step I take, I imagine Lucas walking alongside me, safely. Never in my wildest dreams did I expect to pass any of my classes, let alone come in second after the School Dux. It's a real pinch-me moment. I don't have any words prepared because just like everyone else, we knew Matilda would be the one speaking to all of us today. But she's not. She graciously bowed down to allow someone like me to take her spot. As my feet motion their way onto the stage, Matilda gives me a reassuring smile, and mouths *you've got this.*

With a subtle cough, I clear my throat away from the microphone but it still echoes across the hall. Mum is sitting in the front row, with a tissue in hand. I hope she's aware that this is unplanned so the tissue may be obsolete in this case. Nonetheless, my eyes reveal a light of happiness, locked with hers, so she knows I'm grateful she's there.

"Hi … Uh … I'm not very good at this. But I'll try my best, the same way I have over the last two years. Matilda, thank you for your kindness. Congratulations on your achievements."

I clear my throat again. My body is heating and my heart is racing so fast it feels like it's about to shoot right out.

"We've made it. The Class of 2017. High school years we'll always remember for many reasons. Years of homework, assignments, getting to know teachers—which ones we'll ask for a recommendation from and which ones to steer clear of—and friendships."

The laugh from the crowd is quickly followed by silence.

"Friends come and go, I'm sure all of us can relate to that. My best friend, Lucas, did just that but not out of choice. If he had the choice, he would come and stay. He left an empty hole in my heart and the last two years have been a rollercoaster of emotions, but Lucas didn't leave the world behind without leaving pieces of him to remember. What he did teach me, I'd like to pass on to everyone here today because, in a world where kindness is hard to come by, we can all have a little bit of Lucas to sprinkle around.

"Lucas reminded me how important it is to incorporate our five senses to change the way we view things, especially when our minds start to change gear into negatives because reality is, we'll be facing a lot more challenges once we leave these familiar grounds and face the *real world*, for real life.

"Let's use our eyes to see. The person sitting next to you right now, look at them. Remember them. Because today may be the last time you meet again. Tomorrow they may be halfway across the globe.

"Let's use our sense of touch to feel the beauty of each other. Is that person's hand trembling? Let's hold one another. Place your hand on theirs. Because today may be the last time you get to provide them with warmth. Tomorrow they may be off to a different pathway to yours.

"Let's use our hearing to listen and exchange words of comfort and encouragement. Say just one word, so that person can hold onto it for the years to come. Any word. And then listen to their reply. Because today may be the last time you get to share your thoughts and hear about theirs. Tomorrow they may be on a one-way ticket to the world.

"Let's use our taste to remind someone how tasteful life can be. It doesn't need to be exciting or adventurous on a daily basis, but there are hidden gems throughout our day, you just need to put the ingredients together to make a masterpiece of a dish. Make it memorable. Because today may be the last time you get to put your chef hat on for them. Tomorrow they may be wandering along different roads to you.

"And lastly, let's use our sense of smell to evoke a lasting memory. I'm sure I'm not alone in saying all the Impulse sprays after every P.E. class have left us with a lasting headache. I guess that's the smell of our teenage years. I know it sounds completely odd now, but one day we'll miss that oh so divine smell. So everyone, feel free to spray the heck out of your bottles. Before the wind sweeps it away. Because today may be the last time you get a whiff of that infamous Merely Musk. Tomorrow the smell may be gone forever.

"Today, right now, we have a choice. To leave the same memorable imprint in someone's heart. If not today, then when?"

Everyone claps and to my surprise, there's a standing ovation. Mum's tissue is well used but she continues to wipe away at her cheekbones, where her tears have landed. Happy tears, I hope. Both Stacey and Ali hug me as I walk off the stage and their embrace at this exact moment is one I'll cherish forever, even if tomorrow we go our separate ways.

Ivy and Lea pass us, arms linked as usual, but there's kindness in their eyes. They still don't say a word, but I take it as a good sign that they haven't. Sometimes silence is better than hearing hurtful words. I smile even though it's not reciprocated but it doesn't bother me because maybe it's the gesture they never knew they needed.

"So this is it," Ali sighs. "It doesn't feel real."

Stacey replies, "Yep. Just like that, we'll be off into what everyone calls the real world. Was the last six years not real?" she jokes.

I take in this moment, observing the mixed emotions in their faces and I wonder whether I have the same expression. My heart is still pounding from the speech I just presented but I'm proud of myself for being able to articulate words into sentences without any practise. I'm still convincing myself it happened.

"Congratulations, Wynter." Miss Xi extends her arms for a hug.

"Thank you. I can't believe this is our last day."

"You should be very proud of yourself, Wynter. Those words you shared, they were from the heart. Thank you. It was a good reminder for us adults too."

"I'll miss our weekly chats, but I'm sure a Wynter 2.0 will be knocking on your door somewhere down the road. There'll be many of them and you'll do what you do best. You'll make someone learn to smile again."

Miss Xi wipes away her tears and leans in for another hug. "Don't forget to visit," she says. "I'll be expecting one ... or two."

I don't have to reply because she knows I will. Mum snaps a photo of Miss Xi and I. Ara's standing next to Mum and she praises her for her efforts in taking a photo without any pre-planning.

We all glee in appreciation as Mum takes another stolen shot, acknowledging and praising her for how quickly she's grasping the concept of it. I take two steps towards her and take the Polaroid.

"And this, Mum, is called a selfie. Ready? Say cheese!"

With confusion, Mum quickly says 'cheese' and doesn't expect me to take the photo using my hand and the camera facing us. The photo prints and Mum shakes it so that we can see how it turned out.

"It's perfect," Mum says.

"Picture-perfect," I reply.

30

Map

3 Years Later: 2020

It's Lucas' 5th year death anniversary today. I drive to the all too familiar home that Lucas grew up in and I'm welcomed by Junior and Cora. Just like every year, they know to expect me. They know I'll be there, the same way Lucas knew I'd be there for him for all the years to come.

"It's so nice to see you again, Wynter. It's been too long. We need to see each other more than once a year," Cora says.

"How are things?" I ask, noticing subtle changes in their home. The many framed photographs hang against a feature wall, filled with family photos, particularly from when Lucas and Guy were a lot younger. I'm drawn to their baby photos and struggle to differentiate the two apart. They were both chubby with the biggest dimples.

Junior replies, "We have our good and bad days. But we've got each other to keep ourselves on track."

"And Guy? Is he back from his trip around Asia?"

"He gets back at the end of the year. He's teaching in Japan now. He'll be staying here for two weeks in November."

"That's so good! The kids there must love him. He's always been so gentle and patient with little ones. A quality he and Lucas both shared."

"Ah yes," Cora says. "If you've got a child bursting with big emotions, Guy will be able to help calm them. It's his superpower."

I swallow deeply after hearing the word *superpower*. It makes my heart cheerful for the memory but aches for the longing to see Lucas in the flesh again.

"It's a shame we keep missing each other. We need to try and make our schedules align somehow."

"We'll be sure to let Guy know."

Cora makes me a coffee. Over time I've come to appreciate the taste of it and I can't survive a morning without one now.

As I sit by their dinner table, Salt pounces and then rests quietly by my feet.

"She's always liked you," Cora points out.

I'm taken aback, remembering how Lucas chose Salt's name.

"Salt and Pepper still go on daily walks together, but Ara's probably kept you in the loop with that."

"It's just how Lucas would have liked it," I say. "I wish I could spend longer in town but it's all the annual leave I have left. Plus, Stacey will drag me over there herself if I don't return to work. She complains each work day feels a lot longer without me. But I'm sure it's just her way of saying she misses our chats." I take a brief moment to let my mind wander, "And, I'm still saving up to travel."

"And visit every library around the world?" Junior adds to my words. "Lucas once told us your plans. He had a map and everything. It's good to hear your plans haven't changed."

"At least I'll have Guy to point me to all the best bookstores and libraries around Japan when I finally make my way around Asia. Hopefully, I won't feel so lost or out of place."

"We sure do miss our son, but he loves Japan so much. It wouldn't surprise us if he found a bride and settled down there."

"Gives you an excuse for a holiday," I say. "I've heard so many great things about Japan. Food is just the beginning."

"Speaking of food, come and join us for dinner. I've cooked my specialty, beef lasagne, and Junior's famous sugar bread is in the oven."

"That would be wonderful, thank you. I've missed the taste of homemade sweet bread. Store-bought ones just aren't the same. No wonder the room smells delightful."

Cora sets the table as Junior heads upstairs, slowly but with intention. They're both older and frailer now, but they want to stay in the same two-storey family home where both Lucas and Guy spent most of their childhood years in.

When Junior returns downstairs he has a piece of paper in his hand.

"I found it," he announces, eager to show us.

And then the bell rings.

"Are you expecting anyone?" Cora asks Junior, confused.

The bell rings again. And then both Cora and Junior share a laugh.

"Only one person can be that excited to be home." Junior races for the door like a small child running towards a water park.

As the silhouette that once made it hard for me to breathe walks in, everything moves in slow motion. Sandwiched between Junior and Cora's hug, Guy looks at me with slight embarrassment, but he quickly shrugs it off, knowing how much they've missed him. Cora stamps his cheeks with endless kisses and Junior scruffs his hair, the same way he would with Lucas.

When Guy is set free, we lock eyes from across the room as he walks towards me with arms spread wide. Our faces light up at the shared moment of surprise. Salt wags her way past me and leaps straight into Guy's arms. When he places Salt back down, she remains by his feet, following his every step.

"It looks like someone beat me to that hug," I joke, as Guy now leans in for what feels like our very first embrace.

"I'm glad you're here," Guy says. "It always feels complete."

"Thanks, Guy, I always feel so welcome when I'm in your home. It's such a pleasant surprise seeing you back home, too. It's been way too long!"

Cora and Junior motion for us to continue our conversation in the living room, with a plate of Junior's sugar bread to keep our bellies full and satisfied.

"You've come at the perfect time, Guy. I was just about to show Wynter this."

Junior places the paper on the coffee table and it's the sting to my heart I wasn't expecting. Years have gone by, but traces of Lucas still aches in my heart, especially when they're new traces that I haven't been faced with before.

"Wow," I say. "He did this?"

"He sure did but what's more surprising is how neat it is."

I laugh because his handwriting is readable this time. It's far from messy or reminiscent of a Doctor's script.

"Now you don't need to worry about making a map of your own," Cora says as she admires Lucas' work. "Keep it, sweetheart. It's yours now."

This time, I don't wipe away my tears. I've learned to accept that it's okay to put your raw emotions on a platter. Lucas never shied away from his and it was a quality about him that I admired.

Every teardrop is that of both happiness and sadness. I still miss Lucas, especially his unstoppable spirit to fulfil his dreams. Our dreams.

With a map detailing every bookshop and library around the world that has made it on his list, I make a mental note to make our dream come true.

One day at a time, slowly but surely, I'll check each one of these off.

The rest of the evening in the Mensah home is filled with laughter and tears, stories about Lucas, his childhood highlights, reminiscing our favourite memories together ... and a whole lot of sugar bread.

***

The door couldn't swing open any faster as the doorbell chimes. It's still the same two-note ring. Mum's face glows as bright as the full moon as she envelops me in her arms, with Pepper squeezing between our legs for some warmth. She holds me by the shoulders, taking the moment to soak in every inch of me. There's pure joy in her smile, and the crow's feet around her eyes enhance her natural ageing beauty.

I spend the evening within the four walls I know all too well.

"Oh, sweetie, I've missed you. You look good."

"I've missed you too, Mum."

"Tell me everything. How's work, friends ... What's new?"

"I'm loving every moment of work. Especially shifts with Stacey. Plus, who wouldn't want to walk into a bookstore every morning? And I found out earlier today, it's one on Lucas' list of book places to visit." It takes a few seconds for my words to sink in, before I gaze into the distance with a smile stitched from cheek to cheek.

"I'm so proud of you, sweetie. Lucas would have been too."

"Thanks, Mum."

"And Ara, oh sweetie, Ara is beyond proud of you. She doesn't know you're back. She'll have the biggest shock of her life when she wakes up tomorrow morning. She had a long shift at work so crashed as soon as she got home an hour ago."

"I still can't believe she's a nurse. She used to squirm at the sight of needles. Now she's the one stabbing them."

"Administering," Mum corrects. The word stabbing makes her feel squeamish herself.

We share a deep inhale, happy for this time together, before we call it a night so that Mum can get some rest.

As I make my way upstairs, I'm greeted by a new array of greenery. I close the door slowly behind me, knowing it'll squeak if I pull it too quickly. Ara's room is right next to mine, so I tiptoe quietly. Looking around, I admire the same bedroom that has cradled me in moments of bliss and times of absolute despair. My chest sinks and rises with ease. The room still has the same aura, as though I haven't left at all. It's comforting.

The neatly laid out doona on my old springy mattress is nostalgic, especially when Pepper makes himself comfortable by snuggling into the pillows. But it's what lays flat across my desk on the other end of the room that causes my eyes to well up.

My beloved keyboard.

I walk over and brush my fingers over the dust-covered keys, steadying my movement as I hold the first chord to *Dear Wynter*. The melody carries on deep within my heart—it always has and always will.

I begin to reflect on how far I've come with processing grief and coming to terms with losing my best friend. How difficult it's been. The constant wave of emotions, of extreme highs and lows. How I still have a longing to see Lucas again, but I've learned to take footsteps into this big world without his harmonising with mine. To let go when missing Lucas aches and allow the tears to flow. But to smile and feel excitement when the stars shine a little brighter. It's okay, I remind myself. To feel it all. For sorrow and happiness to co-exist.

It's okay.

Time was cruel to steal Lucas away so early but time has now been my friend, too. Each second ticking around the clock is helping me hurt less. There's still a scar, but it no longer stings the same way as the rawness of a once-open wound. It's the many flashbacks of being with Lucas, the memories I hold onto, that keeps my tears at bay. Without them, I wouldn't find myself smiling out of the blue.

I'll forever miss you Lucas.

Sitting cross-legged next to Pepper, I steady my laptop in front of me, and open a new blank document. It's time to share a story. A beautiful memory ... of the many wondrous, loving, pieces of you, Lucas. A story I can write from the core of my heart so that our friendship can live on, even if only through words.

My fingers hit the keys ...

Everyone seems to be less anxious than I am about the first day of Year 7.

Playlist

I listened to a lot of songs while writing this novel. *Pieces of You* is heavily inspired by the beauty of music and the journey a melody can take us on. Here are the songs that remind me of Wynter and Lucas' story.

1. Dear Wynter – Lucas Mensah

2. Square One – Wynter Hope

3. I'm Only Me When I'm With You – Taylor Swift

4. You Are The Reason – Calum Scott

5. Love You Still – Tyler Shaw

6. Long Long Way To Go – Def Leppard

7. When We Were Young – Adele

8. There You'll Be – Faith Hill

9. My Heart Will Go On – Celine Dion

10. Fix You – Coldplay

11. I'll Never Love Again – Lady Gaga

12. Tonight – FM Static

Acknowledgements

I began the journey of writing my YA novel in 2012 during my work lunch breaks. However, it only got as far as being a saved draft, far from complete. Life introduced its share of twists and turns, delaying the completion of my novel, but it was during those precious years I was able to refine my story writing skills. Fast-forward to 2024, I made a commitment to prioritise my writing, and finally, I wrote the very last word of the very last sentence of my very first novel.

Pieces Of You is inspired by my deep love for music and the profound bonds of friendship. Although the characters and events are purely fictional, I stepped into their shoes, to dig deep into their minds. To bring them to life.

The whole idea of this novel is to explore the theme of love, challenging the conventional notion that romantic love is paramount during high school. *Pieces of You* acknowledges platonic love and the value of true friendship.

I am immensely grateful to everyone who has supported me throughout this entire process. Your words of encouragement, keeping me accountable, and celebrating milestones, kept me going.

To my husband, Trong, although you're not one to read novels, you never stopped believing in me and my dream of holding my own published novel. Thank you.

To my incredible cheer crew, Abigail, Daisy, and Jeremy. Who knew little kids would love a chapter book as much as I loved writing it? Your excitement when asking to read 'just one more chapter' each night before bed is more encouraging than you can imagine. I love that although this story is beyond your years, you still seek more of it.

My parents, Gerry and Delia, deserve a world of thanks for instilling in me a love of reading and writing from a young age. From being inspired to seeing my mum read many books in one night, to my dad happily lending me his typewriter to let my creative thoughts flow.

To my siblings, Gledelyn, Gaizle, Gennie, and Gerald, thank you for always sharing my excitement. You're all so supportive and have inspired me in more ways than you know. Gennie, thank you for basically being my cheerleader from day one and reading all my 'drafts' that remain as that. You've helped me grow as a writer. Gerald, thank you for composing the musical piece for *Dear Wynter* and bringing the lyrics to life.

A heartfelt thanks to my beta readers: Jonathan, Gennie, Rochelle, San, Bertha, and Lorraine. It means so much to me that you took the time out of your busy schedules to read my novel. Your honest feedback was crucial in refining my novel to its final form.

To my Editor, Callie. I can't express enough how amazing it's been working with you. Your expertise and insight have been key to the elevation of my story. You've looked after my debut book with passion, and for that I am eternally grateful.

To my proofreader, Chloe. Thank you for meticulously ensuring every line of my manuscript has been written to perfection and polished for publication. It's not a completed novel without this final check. Thank you.

To Ann, my book cover artist. Your artwork is beautifully hand-drawn and brings my book to life in a captivating and spectacular way. Thank you.

To Frankie, the real-life Pepper. Even though you can't read, thank you for waddling your way through the biggest hike of your life and helping me to better see life through the eyes of a sweet, little Dachshund.

And finally, to you, my reader. Thank you for reading my debut novel. I hope *Pieces of You* resonates with you, offering both enjoyment and reflection. From the bottom of my heart—thank you.

About the author

Glaiza is a self-confessed bookworm with a love for Young Adult novels as they spark relatability and a sense of comfort. If she's not reading, you'll find her playing the guitar, bushwalking, watching a movie, or spending time with the family.

Ever since her teenage years, Glaiza has been an aspiring novelist. *Pieces of You* is her debut novel, a contemporary fiction written to fill the gap of Young Adult novels without the romantic element. Glaiza believes that there is still a captivating story to be told about the beauty of a genuine and lasting friendship.

Glaiza writes from the comfort of her home in Western Sydney, where she grew up. Writing for Glaiza is a way to share her imaginative thoughts and bring relatable characters to life ... All through a world of written words.